The Mystery of the Coughing Dragon

Alfred Hitchcock and
The Three Investigators

in

The Mystery of the Coughing Dragon

Text by Nick West

Based on characters created by Robert Arthur

Armada

First published in the U.K. in 1971 by
William Collins Sons & Co. Ltd., London and Glasgow.
First published in Armada in 1974 by
Fontana Paperbacks,
14 St. James's Place, London SW1A 1PF.

This impression 1978

Printed in Great Britain by
Love & Malcomson Ltd., Brighton Road,
Redhill, Surrey.

Contents

Introduction by Alfred Hitchcock

THIS INTRODUCTION is solely for the purpose of acquainting latecomers with The Three Investigators. If you have met them before, you are under no obligation to read it.

The Three Investigators are an enterprising firm of youthful detectives, amateurs perhaps, but remarkably effective in achieving their goal, namely, solving mysteries.

By his own admission, Jupiter Jones is the leader-in-residence and the brains of the trio. Pete Crenshaw, the most athletic member, assists on missions that call for his kind of contribution. Bob Andrews is in charge of Records and Research. All together, a lively team.

The boys reside in Rocky Beach, a small town some miles from Hollywood, close to the Pacific Ocean. Their headquarters is a converted mobile home trailer located in the Jones Salvage Yard, which is run by Jupiter's aunt and uncle. The trailer has a small office, a lab, a darkroom and equipment which the boys rebuilt from junk in the yard. It can be entered by certain secret passages that are best negotiated by youthful individuals.

Now that you know all that is needed, I shall remove myself from the premises so that you may get on with the real entertainment.

ALFRED HITCHCOCK

1

Mysterious Beginnings

"I WONDER," Jupiter Jones said one morning, "how we would go about attempting the biggest robbery ever seen in this area."

His two companions reacted with surprise. Bob Andrews dropped the stack of small cards he was feeding into their old printing press. Pete Crenshaw, who was mending an old radio, jerked and saw his screwdriver glance off in an erratic arc.

"What was that you said?" Pete asked, trying to smooth out the jagged scratch he'd made on the wooden back of the radio.

"I said I wonder how we would go about attempting the biggest robbery ever tried in this area," Jupiter repeated. "That is, if we were master criminals."

"While you're wondering," Pete said, "try to find out what happens to us after we get caught. I heard somewhere that crime doesn't pay."

Bob Andrews picked up the scattered cards he had dropped. "I don't think we'd be good at being master criminals. I can't even master putting cards into this printing press."

"It was merely a thought," said Jupiter. "After all, we are investigators. It occurs to me that if we could imagine a well-planned crime, we'd be ahead when it came to solving it. All we need to do is reverse our thinking and assume the anti-social mind of a master-mind criminal."

Pete nodded. "That's a neat idea, Jupe. But first I've got to reverse the thinking of the last owner of this radio. He tried to mend it himself and got the wires all twisted. After that, I'll be willing to play mastermind games with you."

The three boys, who called themselves The Three Investigators, were in Jupiter's workshop section of the Jones Salvage Yard. Secluded here, under a six-foot roof extending from the junk yard's high fence, they worked on repairing junk that Jupiter's Uncle Titus bought. They used part of the profits for pocket money and part for such luxuries as the telephone in their secret headquarters.

Pete finished tightening a screw on the radio and held it up proudly for Jupiter's inspection. "This job ought to be worth at least three dollars to your uncle," he said. "Now he can sell it as a working radio instead of the piece of busted junk it was when it came in here."

Jupiter smiled. "Uncle Titus isn't given to throwing his money about carelessly. I suggest you try it first and see if it works."

Pete shrugged and snapped a small dial. "It works, all right," he said. "Listen."

The radio hummed, spluttered and came to life. An announcer's voice was heard, apparently well into his news broadcast. "Authorities continue to be stumped," he said, "over the mysterious happenings in Seaside. Within the past week, five dogs have been reported missing. The pet owners are puzzled over the disappearance of their animals. . . . Now, for news overseas, we take you to—"

"Turn it off, Pete," Jupiter said.

Pete switched the dial to off. "How about that?" he said. "Five missing dogs. Evidently there's a mad dognapper on the loose."

"I think we've got the master criminal Jupe was talking about," Bob said, grinning. "He's going to steal all the dogs he can and corner the market. Then, when people are willing to meet his price, he'll unload and make a fortune."

Jupiter sat pinching his lower lip, a sign that his mental machinery was moving into high gear. "Odd," he said finally.

"What's odd?" Bob asked. "You mean the number of dogs stolen? Five is a good odd number, all right."

Jupiter shook his head, frowning. "No, I was referring to the dogs reported missing within the week. Usually when pets disappear, it happens at irregular intervals, rather than within the short span of one week."

"Well, it must be like I said," Bob answered. "There's this master criminal loose with this mad plan of getting control of the doggie market. Maybe he intends knocking down the price of hamburger meat, in addition to selling the stolen dogs at a handsome profit."

Jupiter smiled thinly. "Nice try. But it doesn't answer the question. Why five missing dogs in one week? Another question is, why haven't we been contacted to investigate these mysterious disappearances?"

"Perhaps they're not so mysterious," Pete said. "Sometimes dogs roam away from home and it takes them longer to get back. That's my guess."

"I agree with Pete," Bob said. "The report didn't mention the dogs being valuable. Just five missing dogs."

Jupiter nodded slowly and reluctantly. "Perhaps you two are right," he admitted. "It may be just a freak coincidence, much as I dislike making such an assumption."

The other two boys smiled. It was Jupiter's habit of using long words whenever possible, apart from his keen deductive abilities as an investigator, that endeared him to them and made him the acknowledged leader of the three.

"I wonder," said Jupe, "how we can solve the mystery without being asked to by any of the pet owners."

Bob and Pete looked at each other blankly. "What mystery?" Pete demanded. "I thought we agreed it was just a freak happening, not a mystery."

"Perhaps," Jupiter said. "But we are investigators, and Seaside is south of here, not too far away. Apparently our fame as investigators is less than we imagined. We should do something about it."

Bob motioned to the stack of cards he had placed in the old printing press. "That's just what I'm doing, Jupe," he said. "Printing new business cards. A fresh batch."

"A good idea, Bob," Jupiter said. "But I was thinking of something else. We will have to be better known, so that when strange things happen, people will think immediately of The Three Investigators of Rocky Beach, California."

Bob threw up his hands. "Well gosh, Jupe, how do you propose doing that? We can't afford to take a TV commercial or hire sky writers."

"I know," Jupiter said. "I suggest we go immediately to Headquarters and have a meeting to discuss ways and means of getting the name of The Three Investigators known to more people."

He got up immediately without waiting for an answer. Bob and Pete exchanged looks, shrugged and followed.

"What I like about you, Jupe," Pete said, smiling, "is the democratic way you run things. I mean, the way we always take a vote before deciding on anything."

The boys moved a piece of old iron grating hidden by the printing press, uncovering the mouth of a large section of corrugated pipe. They crawled into it, replaced the grating, then went forward on hands and knees about forty feet. The pipe went underground some of the way, then ran between some nondescript iron beams. It opened at the other end directly under the mobile trailer which the boys had converted into Headquarters. When Jupiter's uncle, Titus Jones, found he couldn't sell the old trailer, he had given Jupiter and his friends permission to use it.

The boys pushed a trap-door upwards and scrambled through. Then they were inside a tiny office fitted with a desk, a few chairs, a typewriter, filing cabinet and a telephone. Jupiter had connected a microphone and radio loudspeaker to the telephone, which permitted the boys to listen to any phone conversation together. The remainder of the trailer consisted of a tiny darkroom, a miniature lab and a washroom.

Because the trailer was surrounded by piles of junk outside, it was dark inside. Pete switched on the light over the desk.

At that moment the telephone rang.

The boys looked at one another. Hardly anyone ever phoned them.

After the second ring, Jupiter reached for it, switching on the little radio loudspeaker.

"Jupiter Jones?" asked a woman's voice. "Alfred Hitchcock is calling."

"Wow!" Bob yelled. "Maybe he has another good case for us!" Ever since Mr Hitchcock, the famous film director, had learned of The Three Investigators, he had put them on several cases.

13

"Hello, young Jones!" It was Mr Hitchcock speaking. "Are you and your friends busy on a case at the moment?"

"No, sir," Jupiter said. "But according to the law of averages we should find something interesting soon."

Mr Hitchcock chuckled.

"Law of averages, indeed!" he said. "If you're not busy, I have something for you. An old film director friend of mine can use some help."

"We'd be glad to try, Mr Hitchcock," Jupiter said. "What is your friend's problem?"

Mr Hitchcock hesitated, as if he were trying to sum up a difficult situation in a few words.

"It appears to be dog trouble," he said finally. "That is to say, he told me on the telephone a little while ago that his dog is missing."

Jupiter's eyes brightened. "Would your friend happen to be a resident of the town of Seaside, Mr Hitchcock?" he asked.

There was a brief silence.

When Mr Hitchcock came on again, he sounded thunderstruck. "He does live in Seaside, for a fact, young Jones. Now how on earth did you deduce that?"

"Merely putting a few odd occurrences together," Jupiter said.

"Remarkable," Mr Hitchcock was saying. "Quite remarkable, really. I'm pleased that you are still alert and not permitting your organization to become stagnant with conceit and boredom."

Jupiter grinned. "Not a chance, Mr Hitchcock. But you said that your friend 'appears' to be having dog trouble. You put stress on the word 'appears,' sir. Was that your intention?"

"As a matter of fact," Mr Hitchcock said, "you have

guessed quite accurately what I was intending to communicate. I don't believe this is an ordinary case, at all. When you think of it, no case that involves a dragon can be considered ordinary. Wouldn't you agree?"

Jupiter cleared his throat. "A dragon?"

"Yes, my boy. My friend's house overlooks the ocean, and there are caves running beneath it. The night that his dog disappeared, my friend insists he saw a rather large dragon emerge from the ocean and enter one of the caves underneath his dwelling."

There was a stunned silence.

"Well, what do you say, my boy? Are you and your companions willing to try to unravel this mystery?"

Jupiter was so excited, he started to stutter. "J-j-just give me your friend's name and address, sir!" he said. "This sounds as if it could be our most exciting case!"

He wrote down the information Mr Hitchcock gave, promised to report all progress, and hung up. He looked at Pete and Bob triumphantly.

"Anything about a dragon living in our times should be investigated. Don't you agree?"

Bob nodded. Pete shrugged.

"You seem to have some reservations, Pete," Jupiter said.

"You made only one mistake," Pete said. "You told Mr Hitchcock it could be our most exciting case."

"Well, yes, I did," Jupiter replied. "Don't you agree?"

"Not entirely," Pete said.

"What would you have said, then?"

"As long as there's a dragon in it," Pete said, "I would have said—this could be our *last* case!"

2

Horror from the Sea

THE TOWN OF SEASIDE, where Mr Hitchcock's film director friend lived, was about twenty miles away along the Pacific Coast Highway. Hans, one of the two Bavarian yard helpers, had a collection and delivery to make in the area after lunch. Jupiter got permission from his Aunt Mathilda to be taken along with his friends in the small junk yard truck.

Jupiter's aunt fed them all, and then they hurried out and piled into the front with Hans. Jupiter gave him the address, and they were soon on the smooth Coast Highway travelling south.

"You've had time for a little research, Bob," Jupiter said. "What can you tell us about dragons?"

"A dragon," Bob said, "is a mythical monster, usually represented as a large reptile with wings and claws, breathing out fire and smoke."

"I haven't done any research," Pete interrupted. "But I think Bob left out something important. Dragons are not friendly."

"I would have mentioned that, too," Bob said, "but Jupiter is interested only in facts. Dragons are mythical, which means they aren't real. So if they aren't real, we don't have to worry if they're friendly or not."

"Exactly," Jupiter said. "Dragons are creatures of the legendary past. If there ever were any actual ones, it would seem they've all been eliminated by the due processes of evolution."

"That's fine with me," Pete said. "So, if they've all been eliminated, how come we're on our way down to investigate one?"

"We heard that five dogs have disappeared within the past week in the peaceful town of Seaside," Jupiter said. "And Mr Hitchcock told us that a friend of his lost his dog and saw a dragon near his house. Doesn't that suggest anything to you?"

"It sure does," said Pete. "It suggests I should be back in Rocky Beach surfing on my board instead of coming along with you to catch a dragon."

"If Mr Hitchcock's friend, Henry Allen, engages our services, then it will be a profitable adventure for The Three Investigators," Jupiter said. "Why don't you try to look at it that way?"

"I'm trying, I'm trying," Pete said.

"Whether there is a dragon or not," Jupiter said, "something mysterious is apparently going on. Soon we will have facts to work with. Meanwhile we'll have to approach the matter with an open mind."

They had reached the outskirts of Seaside, and Hans slowed the truck as he searched for the street number Jupiter had given him. They travelled slowly another mile and then Hans stopped. "I think this is your party, Jupe," he said.

All they could see was high hedges and palm trees. If a house was there, it seemed to be hiding.

Pete spotted the small sign on a white letterbox. "H. H. Allen," he read. "This must be the place."

The boys piled out. "This preliminary investigation should take approximately two hours, Hans," Jupe said. "Can you make your collection and delivery and come back for us then?"

"Sure thing, Jupe," the husky Bavarian said. He waved and swung his truck round to head down a steep road that led to the centre of the town.

"Let's take a quick look round first," Jupiter said. "It may help if we're better orientated when we speak to Mr Allen."

Houses were strung out along the high ridge overlooking the Pacific. The neighbourhood had a lonely, deserted air. They boys walked to a piece of vacant ground next to the film director's house and looked down.

"Looks nice and peaceful," Bob said, regarding the beach below them and the sparkling waters.

"Neat rollers," muttered Pete, watching the surf. "Not much, but pretty good three-footers. I guess later at night, when the tide and breakers start coming in, would be the best time for the dragon. He'd have a lot more cover."

Jupiter agreed. "You're right, Pete. If there *is* a dragon." He craned his head to look below. "Mr Hitchcock said there were caves below. But they can't be seen from this angle. Later, after our interview with Mr Allen, we'll go down there and look them over."

Bob looked at the deserted beach far below them. "How do we get down?" he asked.

Pete pointed to some rickety-looking, white, weather-beaten boards. "Steps going down, Bob. Beats scaling up and down the cliff wall."

Jupiter pointed along the ridge. "There are some other staircases, too. But I don't see many of them. Well, I believe we have the lie of the land. Now let's hear what Mr Allen will tell us."

He led the way back to a gate in the hedge, swung it open, and they all stepped through. Beyond a winding path, they could see a house of faded yellow brick, surrounded by palm trees, bushes and wild flowers. The garden had an air of neglect as did the old house itself, perched almost on the edge of the wind-swept cliff.

Jupiter raised the door knocker and let it fall.

The door opened, and a small plump man stood there. He had large mournful brown eyes, bushy eyebrows, and a fringe of white hair above his tanned and wrinkled face.

"Come in, boys," he said, extending his hand. "I imagine you're the boys my good friend Alfred Hitchcock said might help me. Investigators, are you?"

"Yes, sir," Jupiter said. He whipped out one of The Three Investigators' business cards. "We've solved several cases so far."

The old man looked at the card in his gnarled fingers. It said:

THE THREE INVESTIGATORS

"We Investigate Anything"

?   ?   ?

First Investigator – JUPITER JONES
Second Investigator – PETER CRENSHAW
Records and Research – BOB ANDREWS

"The question marks," Jupiter explained, "are our symbol, our trademark. They stand for questions unanswered, riddles unsolved, mysteries unexplained. We attempt to solve them."

The old man nodded, as if satisfied, and put the card in his pocket. "Come into my study, and we'll talk," he said.

He led them to a large sunny room. The boys gasped as they looked about them. From ceiling to floor, the walls were hung with pictures almost fighting for space. Apart from the many paintings, there were neatly framed autographed photographs of famous film stars and other celebrities.

The large desk was covered with papers and small wooden carvings. The bookcases were crowded, too, with strange artifacts, Pre-Columbian figurines, and small, grotesque African figures. Some of them looked cruel and frightening.

The old man indicated three chairs for them and took the large carved chair behind the desk. "Please sit down, boys, and I'll tell you why I called my old friend Alfred Hitchcock. Perhaps he has already told you that I am a film director?"

"Yes," said Jupiter. "He mentioned that, sir."

The old man smiled. "*Was* would be a better word for it. I haven't done anything for many years. I was a film director years before Alfred became one. And quite famous in my own right, too. While Alfred has made the Hitchcock thriller his own speciality, I had mine, too. Almost in the same vein, but slightly different. Alfred concerns himself with logical mysteries of the real world, but mine went beyond it."

"What do you mean, sir?" Jupiter asked.

"It will explain why I couldn't go to the police or other authorities with my problem. You see, my pictures were bizarre, of the world beyond, of nightmares and fright. They concerned themselves with monsters, werewolves, creatures of strange and hideous natures and violent emotions.

"In short, my speciality, boys, was the horror film!"

Jupiter nodded. "Yes, I remember your name now, sir. I've seen it at film festivals in museums."

"Good," said the old man. "So when I tell you about what I saw coming out of the water the night my dog disappeared, you will know why I hesitated to speak about it. With my reputation and my inability to find work for many years, it would be only natural for stupid people to think I was merely trying to attract attention, gain publicity.

"My work is finished. They saw to that—the powers that be. I have enough money to live quietly. And no worries, no fears—except—"

"Except the dragon now living in the cave below you, sir?" Jupiter suggested.

Mr Allen grimaced. "Yes." He looked carefully at the boys. "I told Alfred I saw it coming out of the sea. But I omitted one fact. You see, I *heard* it, too!"

The room became suddenly quiet.

"You heard the dragon," Jupiter said calmly. "Exactly what did you hear? And where were you at that moment?"

Mr Allen drew out a large coloured handkerchief and mopped his brow. "I was standing on the cliff outside my house looking down at the ocean when I saw it," the old man said. "Perhaps it was an illusion."

"Perhaps," Jupiter said. "Now tell us exactly what you heard. This might be an important lead in the mystery."

"Well, confound it," Mr Allen said. "As far as I know, there aren't any dragons around, and there haven't been for several million years. Of course, I've done pictures about them, using mechanical monsters. In those cases, we used some kind of muffled roar of an engine combined with shrill whistles, blended together to create the effect we were trying to achieve—that of frightening the audience.

"But what I heard last night wasn't anything like

that at all. It was rather a high-pitched rasping sound—almost as if it were breathing with difficulty—or coughing."

"What about the cave under your house?" Jupiter asked. "Is it large enough to contain a dragon, or any creature large enough to be mistaken for one?"

"Yes," the old man said. "There are a series of caves running under this ridge. Extending north and south as well as inland. In the old days, they were used by rum-runners, and before them by smugglers and pirates. There was a landslide some years ago as the cliffs eroded, covering much of what was known then as Haggity's Point. But many of the caves are still under here."

"Hmmmm," Jupiter muttered. "But this is the first time you've ever seen or heard a dragon, and yet you've been living here for years. Is that correct?"

The old man nodded and smiled. "Once is enough. And I might not even have seen this one if I hadn't been out looking for my dog, Red Rover."

The boys exchanged glances, smiling. One of their secret entrances into Headquarters was called Red Gate Rover.

"I guess it's time we discussed your missing dog and the circumstances, sir. Bob, take notes," Jupiter said.

Bob, in charge of Records and Research, took out his pad and pencil.

Mr Allen started, then smiled at this example of the business-like proficiency of The Three Investigators.

"I've been abroad for the past two months," he said. "Even though I am no longer actively working in films, I am still very much interested in them, and their development. As a rule I tour Europe ever year, going to most of the major film festivals in different foreign cities. This year was no different. I went to the festivals in Rome, Venice, Paris, London and Budapest, and also visited old friends.

"As usual, when abroad, I boarded my dog at a local kennel. I returned a week ago, got Red Rover out—he's an Irish setter, by the way—beautiful animal. Friendly, too.

"Red Rover likes to run. As I can't keep up with him, I let him loose at night. Two nights ago he didn't return. Although I've had him three years, I thought he'd picked up new habits and returned to the kennel. I called and he wasn't there. I waited for him to come back and he didn't.

"I was out looking for him—when I saw—*it!*"

"You didn't go down to the beach?" asked Jupe.

The old man shook his head. "No. It was an eerie sensation. I'd spent most of my life making pictures to shock and scare people out of their wits, and now it had happened to me. There's no way I can describe the feelings I had. Panic, first, that this awesome creature might have attacked and devoured my dog. Then the fear that I might be losing my mind. To admit openly that you have seen a dragon takes some doing, believe me!"

"You took no other steps then," pursued Jupiter, "but phoned your friend Alfred Hitchcock."

The old man mopped his brow again. "Alfred is an old and dear friend, with much experience in the field of mystery. I knew if anybody could help me, he was the one. Now it will be up to you boys. The entire matter is in your hands."

"Thank you, Mr Allen," Jupiter said, "for your confidence. There have been other incidents of missing dogs in this town. Five of them, at last report, not including yours."

Mr Allen nodded. "I heard that on the news after my dog had disappeared. If I had heard of it before, I might not have let Red Rover run on his own as I did."

"Have you spoken to the other dog owners?" Jupiter asked.

The old man shook his head. "No. Not yet. I didn't want to mention what I'd seen."

"Do all the people round here own dogs?"

Mr Allen smiled. "Not all. Not the man across the street, Mr Carter. Nor my next-door neighbour on the right, Arthur Shelby. I don't know many of my neighbours. I live a quiet life with my books and paintings. And my dog."

Jupiter stood up. "We'll be going then, Mr Allen, and I promise you a full report of any progress we make."

Mr Allen shook hands and saw them out, thanking them again. The boys went out through the wooden gate, and Jupiter closed it behind them.

Pete smiled as Jupiter set the hook in place. "Keeping out the dragon, Jupe?"

"I doubt very much that a mere locked gate, or even a locked door, would stop a dragon, Pete," said Jupiter.

The Second Investigator gulped nervously. "I don't like the way you said that," he declared. He looked up the street, and then glanced at his watch. "Where's Hans?"

"It's much too early," Jupiter said. "We still have plenty of time."

He started to walk across the street.

Bob and Pete looked at him.

"Time for what?" Bob asked.

"To call on Mr Carter," Jupiter said. "After him,

Mr Arthur Shelby. Aren't you curious about men who live in this lonely section and don't need dogs to protect them?"

"No, I'm not," Pete said. "As a matter of fact, I'm wondering why I haven't bought a dog yet to protect *me!* A large one that's not afraid of dragons!"

Jupiter smiled and the boys followed him to the other side of the narrow street. Mr Carter's grounds were well kept up and his house was freshly painted.

"Notice," Jupiter told his friends as they went up the path, "that the hedges are evenly clipped and the lawn neatly mowed. His trees are pruned and his flower beds are well tended. Mr Carter must be a neat man."

Jupiter pressed the bell. Almost immediately the front door was flung open and a heavyset man stood there glowering down at them.

"Yes? What do you kids want?" he demanded loudly.

"I beg your pardon, sir," Jupiter said politely. "We've just visited your neighbour, Mr Allen, across the street. His dog, Red Rover, is missing, as you may know. We were wondering if you knew anything about its disappearance."

The man's eyes narrowed and his thick eyebrows rose, then lowered. His mouth twisted into a snarling line.

"So Allen's lost his dog, has he? Like the others up the street, eh? Well, good riddance to them. Good riddance and let's hope they stay lost. I hate dogs!"

His eyes blazed furiously at them, with an almost insane glint. His hands clenched and for a moment the boys thought he was going to attack them.

Jupiter managed to keep his voice calm, and his placid-looking exterior unruffled. "I'm sure you must have a good reason for disliking the animals, sir," he said. "Perhaps if you could tell us what they've done—"

"What they've done?" the man echoed sarcastically. "Done what they've always done. Barked and howled at the moon all night. Trampled my flower beds. Ripped up my lawn. Upset my dustbins, littering the path. That enough for you?"

"I'm sorry," Jupe said sympathetically. "We're new to the neighbourhood. It's Mr Allen's dog we're trying to find. If it's damaged your property, I'm sure Mr Allen would pay for it. He misses his dog terribly and I'm sure he'd do anything—"

"Do anything, would be?" the man asked. "Well, so would I. Wait here!"

He ducked inside behind the door. The boys hardly had time to exchange baffled glances than the door was flung open again and Mr Carter was back.

He was holding a large shotgun.

"Here's what I'd do," he said, raging. "Fill him with lead! This one carries double ought. That's the largest ammunition made for this weapon. And if I set eyes on that dog of Allen's or any other pesky beast hereabouts on my property, here's what they'll get."

He raised the gun threateningly.

3

The Test of Terror

THE ANGRY MAN tightened his finger on the trigger. "I'm a good shot and I never miss. Any more questions?"

Jupiter shook his head, trying not to look unnerved by the gun a foot from his face. "No, sir," he said. "I'm very sorry if we have disturbed you. Good day, sir."

Mr Carter's lips tightened. "If I never see any of those pesky dogs around again, that's when it'll be a good day. Now git!"

He thrust the muzzle outwards as he spat out the words, and the boys backed off slowly.

"Turn round," the man said. "I don't want you spoiling my lawn!"

Jupiter looked at his two companions and shrugged. With hearts quaking, they turned their backs on the ill-tempered man with the gun and went down the path.

"Don't run, walk slowly," Jupiter whispered.

Bob and Pete nodded, wondering when the shotgun blast would come, trying not to panic.

Then they all jumped at the loud sound behind them!

"It's all right, fellows," Jupiter said. "That was just Mr Carter slamming his front door."

The boys turned, saw Jupiter was correct, and ran.

They were halfway down the street before they stopped. They looked back. Nobody was after them. Mr Carter's door remained closed.

"Whew!" Bob muttered. "That was close!"

"A shotgun with double-ought ammunition," Pete said, testing his forehead for sweat. "One more second and that stuff would have ripped right through us."

"Not too likely," Jupe said. "The locking bolt was in the off and therefore safe position."

Bob and Pete glared at him. "You knew that all the time," Pete said accusingly. "No wonder you acted so calm."

"I don't believe Mr Carter ever intended to shoot us," Jupiter said. "He was merely acting out his anger. I happened to trigger him off by bringing up the one subject that annoys him. Dogs!"

"I think he's got another subject now," Pete said. "People!"

Jupiter pursed his lips thoughtfully. "We'll have to be more careful the next time we approach Mr Carter."

Pete shook his head. "No, sir. The next time you can be careful approaching Mr Carter all you want. You won't have to worry about me, because I won't be there. I forgot to tell you, I have a very delicate skin. It's allergic to lead."

"Me, too," Bob said. "If I'm going to be shot at, I prefer a water pistol at ten paces."

"There's a possibility," Jupiter said, "that Mr Carter is a far better actor than I give him credit for, and had something to do with the disappearance of the dogs."

"Sounds reasonable," Bob said.

"It will be a simple matter now to compare Mr Carter's irascible response with our next subject's."

"What's he talking about now?" Pete asked Bob.

Jupiter pointed across the street.

"There were two neighbours Mr Allen mentioned who did not own dogs. We met the first one, Carter. Now we have a few questions to ask the other one, Arthur Shelby."

A closed metal gate running chest high barred their way. The boys looked over it to the large house set back on the property of Mr Arthur Shelby.

"Looks okay," Bob said. "I don't see a cannon emplacement anywhere."

Pete inched a little closer to look at the windows on the lower and upper storeys. "I don't see anybody watching us," he said. "Maybe Mr Shelby isn't home."

Jupiter stepped forward. "It's easy to find out," he said. "All we have to do is go through this gate, and—"

He stopped, open-mouthed. His companions gaped too. The gate had opened without Jupiter touching it.

"How did you do that?" Pete demanded. "You developing magical powers?"

"Maybe the wind blew it open," Bob suggested.

Jupiter shook his head. He held out his arms, stopping his companions from advancing, and stepped back. The metal gate swung shut.

Jupiter took a step closer. The gate opened.

"A very simple explanation," he said. "The gate works on an electronic seeing-eye principle. You've all seen that at airports, supermarkets and other modern buildings."

Pete looked at the gate sceptically. "Sure I have," he said. "Only I've never seen one in a private house before."

"Any sign of progress and modernity is a good sign," Jupiter said cheerfully. "The fact that Mr Shelby uses such a device on his gate shows he is not superstitious or hidebound by convention. Just the kind of person we want to talk to, especially about such an unlikely topic as a dragon in the neighbourhood."

He stepped through the gate and the other boys followed. Off to the side of the path, the boys saw a large, ornate sundial set in the centre of the lawn. Ahead of them was a large flower laden trellis. They walked under it.

Suddenly the trellis dropped.

The boys stopped, bumping into each other. The front part of the trellis had dropped in front of them. Behind them, the back part of the trellis hissed downwards with a slight clanging sound, barring their retreat.

They were trapped in a huge metal cage decorated with flowers!

"I hope this is only a joke," Jupiter said, licking his lips nervously. "It's like a portcullis."

"What's a portcullis?" Pete asked in a panicky voice.

"It was usually a large, heavy iron grating suspended by chains and lowered between grooves to bar the gateway of a castle or fortified town," Jupiter explained.

"I've seen pictures of them in old books at the library," Bob said excitedly. "It's usually the last defence after you cross the moat of the castle."

"I don't remember crossing any moat," Pete complained fretfully.

There was a slight hissing sound, and as suddenly as it had fallen, the trellis lifted above their heads.

The boys looked at each other.

"I think Mr Arthur Shelby has a keen sense of humour," Jupiter said, relieved. "Let's go."

He took a step forward and Pete grabbed his arm. "You're going the wrong way, Jupe," he said. "Maybe they don't want us in this castle."

Jupiter shook his head, smiling. "First an automatic-opening gate. Then an electronic controlled trellis. Mr Shelby seems to be unusually preoccupied with scientific gadgets. It would be a shame not to meet him."

The menacing bird dived at the boys!

Jupe moved forward again and his companions followed reluctantly. He grinned as he stepped up and pressed the doorbell.

"Yow-wh!" he yelled, and leaped back, shaking his arm. "That doorbell has an electric charge on it! I got a shock!"

"Okay, I've had enough of this Mr Shelby's jokes," Pete said. "I vote we call off the interview with this joker right away."

"I'm with Pete," Bob said. "I've got a funny feeling Mr Shelby is trying to tell us he doesn't want us here."

"I don't think so," Jupiter said. "He's testing us. He's put us through a sequence calculated to scare us off."

As if in answer to Jupiter's reasoning, the front door clicked and swung silently open.

"Neat," Bob said admiringly. "He's got this place bugged all around."

The boys cautiously stepped over the threshold. The interior was dark and quiet.

Jupiter cleared his throat, trying to speak with confidence. "Good day, Mr Shelby. We are The Three Investigators, calling at the suggestion of your next-door neighbour, Mr Allen. May we come in, sir?"

There was no answer. Then faintly they heard a slight flapping sound. It came closer, and they heard it more distinctly. It appeared to be coming from high in the gloomy interior of the house. Suddenly they froze. A huge, dark form was hurtling towards them with a shrill whistling sound.

A big, black, hawklike bird, screeching fiercely, its sharp beak open, cruel talons outstretched, and eyes blazing madly, swooped down on them!

4

A Surprising Hand

"DUCK!" Pete yelled.

The boys flung themselves to the floor.

The screeching bird plummeted towards them, its huge talons curled menacingly.

Then it slowed to hover a foot above them.

Surprisingly, it remained there.

The shrill screeching sound stopped.

Jupiter had flung his hands over his face to protect his eyes. He peeked cautiously between his fingers. Then he sat up, his expression changed from fear to chagrin.

"It's okay, fellows," he said. "It's not a real bird."

"What?" Pete cried.

He lifted his head unbelievingly. Bob did the same.

The dark bird hung there limply, dangling at the end of a thin copper wire. Its yellow eyes glared at them with a dull expression.

"It's a toy," Jupiter said. He reached out and touched the bird. "Seems to be made out of plastic and chicken wire!"

"Oh, boy!" Pete said disgustedly.

From the dark interior of the room came the sound of rasping, breathless laughter. Lights flashed on suddenly overhead.

A tall, thin man wearing dark overalls stood there looking down at them. His hair was short and coppery red.

"Welcome to Mystery Castle," he said in a deep and sepulchral voice.

Then he doubled over, laughing. His laughter became riddled by a spasm of coughing.

"He's sure got a keen sense of humour," Pete muttered.

The tall, red-headed man straightened up slowly. His blue eyes were bright and watery. "Arthur Shelby here. I'd better take my bird back before it bites you."

The boys scrambled to their feet. The man came closer, stooped and unhooked the wires holding the motionless bird. Jupiter looked up at the ceiling and smiled.

"He had it running on those narrow-gauge tracks up there," he said. "Just like electric toy trains."

Bob and Pete looked up at the tracks stretching across the ceiling. "I like electric trains better," Pete said. "They don't scare me."

Mr Shelby was grinning. "Fooled you, did I? Sorry. It's my hobby—making crazy gadgets," He waved his hand to the room behind him. The boys saw a large workshop cluttered with tools and scraps of wood and wire.

Mr Shelby set his bird down on a work table. His voice was normal now, not deep and mournful, merely husky. "What brings you boys here?" he asked.

Jupiter handed Mr Shelby one of their business cards. "That may explain it, sir," he said. "We like to solve mysteries."

The red-haired man studied the card, making no comment about the question marks. Then he returned it, smiling.

"I suppose the mysteries round here are the missing dogs, eh?"

"When we learn all the facts of the matter," Jupiter said slowly, "it may turn out to be a single mystery. We're trying to help Mr Allen find his Irish setter. But I have a feeling his missing dog is linked somehow with the disappearance of the others in Seaside."

"Could be," Mr Shelby said. "I don't have much to do with my neighbours here but I heard the report on the news. Allen's been away and I wasn't even aware he had come back until I heard Red Rover was missing, too. I hope you find him."

"That's our job," Jupiter said. "But we can use some information. I thought talking to some of Mr Allen's neighbours would help. We've just been across the street to speak to Mr Carter. Do you know him?"

Shelby laughed. "Who doesn't round here? I've got the red hair but Carter has the temper. I suppose he let you see his shotgun?"

Jupiter shrugged. "He tried to frighten us off. Fortunately, he had the safety catch on when he threatened us. He said dogs round here have been trespassing on his property. He made it clear he hates dogs."

Shelby grinned. "Carter hates everything and everybody."

"You scare people off in a different way," Pete said suddenly. "What's the idea of all those tricks you've got set up round your house?"

The red-haired man glanced at Pete, amused. "I wondered when you'd get round to me. I don't hate people so much as I hate to be *bothered* by them. I've worked out a few ways to keep the pedlars and daily nuisances away. Scared you, did I?"

"You can say that again," Pete muttered.

Shelby laughed again. "My background is engineering. I'm an amateur inventor It's fun for me to rig up these gadgets. But nobody gets hurt."

He glanced at his watch. "Now, how can I help you boys?"

"About the missing dogs," Jupiter said, "do you have any ideas that might help us?"

Their host shook his head. "Sorry All I know is they've been reported missing. You'd do better speaking to the owners."

"The only one we've spoken to is Mr Allen next door," Jupiter said. "He gave us a clue but it's kind of hard to believe."

"Oh?" The red-haired man's bushy eyebrows flew upward. "What was that?"

Jupiter pursed his lips, frowning. "The trouble is, I don't know if I'm allowed to tell you about it."

"Why not?" Shelby demanded.

"I think maybe Mr Allen might be embarrassed if word of it got about," Jupiter said. "I'm sorry, Mr Shelby."

The tall man shrugged. "I guess you've got to act like a lawyer in these matters. Protect your client's confidences. Something like that?"

Jupiter nodded. "And yet, it's odd. You live next to him. It doesn't seem likely that he saw something mysterious round here that you didn't see."

Mr Shelby grinned. "You seem to have a pretty good vocabulary. Seems to me you could talk a lot clearer, if you wanted to."

"You're not kidding," Pete said, impatiently. "What Jupe is trying *not* to say is that Mr Allen saw a dragon come out of the ocean the other night."

"You shouldn't have said that, Pete," Jupiter said. "We have to keep what our clients tell us in confidence."

"Sorry," Pete muttered. "I guess I get too nervous just thinking about it."

37

"A dragon?" Mr Shelby said. "Is that what Allen claims he saw?"

Jupiter hesitated. Then he shrugged. "Well, it's out now. I guess he was afraid people would think he was losing his mind if he talked about seeing a dragon. But that's what he claims he saw."

Mr Shelby was shaking his head. "Impossible."

"He said he heard it, too," Bob said. "That is, when it entered the cave under his house."

Jupiter blew out his cheeks. "Well, I guess we just don't keep any secrets at all, Mr Shelby. But if there really is a dragon, or something dangerous like that down there, you ought to know about it, too. I mean, in case you go down there at times."

"Thanks for the warning," Mr Shelby said. "But I rarely go down to the beach. I'm not much of a swimmer, you see. And as for the caves, I learned long ago not to go into them. They're dangerous."

"What makes them dangerous?" Bob asked.

Mr Shelby smiled. "They were dangerous before there was any talk of a dragon in them. Landslides are common here along the coast. You could be buried alive."

"I heard they were used by smugglers and rum-runners," Jupiter said.

Shelby nodded. "That was a long time ago. As for the landslides, just take a walk along the cliff. You'll see how the earth has slipped. Sometimes a house goes down with it."

He looked intently at the boys, his eyes shining. "I know how it is being young. I suppose if I were your age again, and heard a wild story about a dragon, I might be tempted to go down and take a look myself. If you do, remember, those caves are very dangerous."

"Thanks, Mr Shelby," Jupiter said. "Then in your opinion, there's nothing to Mr Allen's dragon?"

Shelby smiled. "What do you think?"

Jupiter threw up his hands. "Well—"

Mr Shelby laughed again.

"Well," Jupiter said, "thanks a lot for talking to us. Maybe we'll find out exactly what he did see."

"I hope so," Mr Shelby said. "I know Allen's made a lot of horror films in his time. Maybe he has a friend or enemy who's playing a practical joke on him."

"That's possible," Jupiter admitted.

"Sometimes people will go to extremes in a case like that. Sorry I can't help you boys. I'll see you out now."

He led them to the door and opened it. As they filed out, he stopped Jupiter, offering his hand. "Good luck, son."

Jupiter took the hand extended to him. "Thank you, sir."

The door closed softly behind him.

Then he stared down open-mouthed, a shiver running through him.

Mr Shelby's right hand had come off, and Jupiter was holding it in his own!

5

Trouble Below!

"ULP!" Jupiter stared, horrified, at Mr Shelby's hand. It was flesh-coloured and looked real. It even *felt* real!

It was too much for even level-headed Jupiter. He gasped and dropped it.

The other investigators heard his cry and turned.

"Yipes! What's that?" cried Pete.

"Whiskers!" Bob said, looking closer. "It's a hand!"

Jupiter found his voice. "It's Mr S-Shelby's. It c-came off when we were shaking hands!"

"What?" Pet asked.

"It came off," Jupiter repeated dully. "I don't know how."

Loud laughter came from inside the house. It was followed by strangling, coughing sounds.

Jupiter flushed. "My fault, guys. I forgot what a practical joker Mr Shelby is."

He picked up the hand gingerly and held it out to Bob and Pete. Pete shook his head, and Bob took it. "It even feels real," Bob said. "Maybe Mr Shelby wears an artificial arm, and his hand just happened to come off accidentally when you shook hands."

Jupiter shook his head. "You heard him laughing a moment ago. No, it's just another one of his practical jokes. That's all. He's got a funny way of scaring people."

"Yeah," Pete said sarcastically. "Very funny. Let's

get out of here before he thinks of something else."

Bob tossed the fake hand away. The boys turned and raced down the walk.

Avoiding Mr Shelby's portcullis, the boys zigzagged across the path. They slowed down as they approached the closed metal gate.

It swung open noiselessly, as before, and The Three Investigators hurried through.

"He's a good sport anyway," Bob said, as they ran down the street. "At least he didn't have his gate bite us on the way out."

"Keep going," Pete muttered. "I'll thank him when I'm far enough away."

Finally they slowed and came to a breathless halt.

"Now what do we do?" Bob asked. "Wait for Hans to pick us up?"

"I move that we keep running all the way back to Rocky Beach," Pete said. "What's twenty miles when you consider how much safer it is there?"

Jupiter plucked at his lower lip. He glanced at his wrist watch. "There's still a little time. How do you fellows feel about taking a quick look at that cave down below, before we go home?"

Pete looked towards the cliff ridge. "You mean the one the dragon's supposed to have gone into? I'll give you my vote in two words, Jupe. Forget it."

Jupiter nodded. "How do you feel, Bob?"

"Like Pete," Bob answered. "Besides, you heard Mr Shelby telling us how dangerous it is. I don't know about the dragon, but I don't think I'd be any happier under a landslide."

Jupiter was walking to the cliff edge. He put his hand on the old weatherbeaten stair handrail that ran steeply down to the beach.

"I suggest we take a look," he said. "Then, when

we get home, we'll have a better idea of what we're up against."

With that, he took a step down and quickly disappeared from view.

Pete looked at Bob. "How come he always outvotes us, one to two?"

Bob shrugged. "He's just more stubborn than we are. You and I are probably nicer people."

"Yeah," Pete muttered. "A lot of good it does us. Come on. We'd better go down after him before Mr Shelby sends a flying object after us. Or that Mr Carter across the street decides he needs some target practice."

With that, Pete reached for the handrail and started down. Bob followed. The steps were narrow and old, set close together, and the descent to the beach was steep. As they ran down, Pete and Bob grabbed the rails at first. Then, as they gained momentum and confidence, they merely reached out and slapped at them.

Jupiter couldn't help but hear the clatter behind him. He glanced back once, saw what was happening, and grinned. It was a race to the bottom now.

Not as agile as the others, Jupe could still make an effort when he wanted to. He increased his pace as he bounced from step to step.

He was perhaps fifteen feet from the bottom when it happened.

Suddenly, without warning, a step collapsed under his weight. His momentum carried him downwards. The next step cracked and broke away, too. He attempted to brake by grabbing the handrail.

It tore loose and came off in his hand. Then he was yelling and fallng in space.

Immediately behind, Bob and Pete heard his warning cry too late. The entire staircase below was collapsing

42

like a deck of cards on end. The railing above the section that Jupiter had clung to was their only chance. They threw themselves at it frantically.

It tore loose, too.

Helplessly, they plunged headlong downwards. Loose boards hurled after them.

Jupiter's mind worked quickly as he fell. In the split second before he landed, he had two nagging thoughts.

Was this accident a real one?

Or was it to keep The Three Investigators from investigating the mystery of the dragon on the beach?

That was all he had time for.

He landed with stunning force. Bodies and boards crashed about his head.

Everything went black!

6

Trapped!

"JUPE, are you all right?"

Jupiter blinked and opened his eyes. He saw the blurred faces of Pete and Bob looking down at him.

He grunted and sat up. There was a lot of sand on his face, and he brushed it off carefully before replying.

"Of course I'm all right," he said finally. "Not that the effect of both of you landing on me at once did me any good. In addition to knocking the breath out of me, you practically buried my face in the sand."

Pete grinned. "He's okay. He can still talk."

"I hear him," Bob said. "As usual, he's making it seem our fault. As I recall, his weight broke the steps and railing first. What were we supposed to do—fly over him?"

Jupiter got to his feet slowly. He kicked at the litter of broken boards all round them. Then he picked up a splintered piece and studied it. He stooped and picked up another, comparing it with the first. He nodded as if satisfied.

"Your statement is correct, Bob," Jupiter said. "My weight did break the steps first. But I'm inclined to believe that I had help. These steps appear to have been tampered with. Enough to make them give way at the slightest pressure."

He extended the boards to his two partners.

"If you notice, the top part is splintered sharply. See how jagged it is? The bottom part is broken more

44

evenly. Almost as if it had been partly sawn through before we came down the steps."

Bob and Pete looked at the boards closely.

"Maybe you're right," Bob admitted. "But who knew we were coming down them?"

"Sure." Pete said. "It was your own idea, Jupe. If we never went down the steps, the accident could have happened to anybody in the neighbourhood. We've only met Mr Carter, Mr Allen and Mr Shelby, so far. There must be a lot of others who use this staircase."

He pointed up the beach. "It's a long walk to the other one. And a longer walk to the next one. Anybody could have come down here."

Jupiter sighed and threw the boards down. "We don't have the equipment to examine these boards anyway, to find out if they were actually sawed or not. Maybe I'm wrong in my deduction."

Pete and Bob stared at each other. It was a rare day when Jupiter ever admitted to a wrong guess about anything.

Jupiter set his lips firmly. "However, " he said, "we can't let ourselves be sidetracked by the accident on the steps. Our main purpose in coming down was to examine the beach here and the cave for evidence of the dragon. Let's get on with it."

Without a backward glance, Jupe started walking towards the sea. "We'll look for tracks leading from the water inland towards the cave first. What Mr Allen claimed he saw took that direction."

Bob and Pete joined him, and the three advanced slowly over the sand. The wide expanse of beach appeared deserted. Overhead a few seagulls, screaming raucously, swooped about in erratic flight.

Pete pointed to one of the gulls who had just landed. "Maybe we ought to ask one of them if he saw a dragon recently. That would save us a lot of trouble."

"Good idea," Bob said. "And if they won't talk, there's that tug with the salvage rig about a mile out."

He pointed offshore to a clumsy-looking craft trailing its rig. "They don't look like they're going anywhere in a hurry. Maybe they're on a dragon hunt, too."

Jupiter looked out and shook his head. "We don't have to worry about what's out that far. All we have to do is cover the shoreline round here."

He ran his eye from the cave in the distance towards the water. "We should see tracks somewhere in this area. I suggest we spread out a little."

They separated and walked slowly along the beach, scrutinizing the sand closely.

"All I see is a lot of seaweed piled up," Bob said.

"Me, too," Pete said. "Plus some seashells and a lot of driftwood."

Bob shook his head finally. "No sign of any kind of tracks, Jupe. Could the tide have washed them away?"

Jupe tugged at his lip. "Possibly here, close to the water. But there's plenty of dry sand for tracks all the way up to the cave. Let's go up and look."

"Do we have to?" asked Pete. "What if the dragon is in the cave? What are we supposed to do—fight it off with our bare hands?"

"I don't expect us to have to fight anything, Pete," Jupe said. "We'll approach the cave entrance carefully. And we won't go inside unless we're certain it's safe enough."

Pete scowled. Then he stooped and picked up a long piece of driftwood. "Well, I don't know how much good this will do me. But I'll feel a lot safer with some kind of club in my hands."

Bob picked up another piece of wood, part of an

46

oar with the blade broken off. "You have the right idea, Pete," he said. "I remember seeing pictures of St George and the dragon. He didn't use old driftwood, either. He was smart. He had a nice long sword."

He brandished his long oar, then glanced at Jupiter. "Don't you want some kind of weapon, too, Jupe? We can go back for those broken railings, if you like. They've still got some of the nails set in them. Nice long ones."

Jupiter smiled and shrugged. "I suppose it won't hurt to carry something."

With that, he reached down and picked up a long, wet plank from the debris along the shore. He put it on his shoulder and glanced at his companions.

Bob and Pete smiled weakly. Then, with resolutely set faces and quaking hearts, the boys walked slowly towards the dark opening in the face of the cliff.

They crossed the slight ridge near the waterline, scanning the sand each foot of the way. Suddenly Jupiter stopped. His eyes were bright.

"Here's something," he said softly.

Bob and Pete looked down. There were unmistakable depressions in the loose soft sand.

"This dragon must be a new type," Bob said finally. "It looks like it's running on wheels."

Jupiter nodded. He looked up and down the beach. "I don't see anything. But these look like the tracks of some kind of vehicle. Maybe a beach buggy. Sometimes lifeguards use a jeep or beach buggy to patrol a long area, such as this."

"Maybe," Bob said. "But if they were on patrol, these tracks would be heading north and south—the way the beach runs. Instead, they're heading towards the cave."

"You're right, Records," Jupiter said. He dropped to his knees and studied the depressions.

Bob was scowling, looking back at the water. "I don't get it. If the tracks show here, why couldn't we see them near the water?"

"A heavy running tide and high breakers would wash them away, I guess," Jupiter said.

Pete grinned. "I guess old Mr Allen's eyes aren't too reliable. Instead of a dragon, what he probably saw was a jeep or something."

"Possibly," Jupiter answered. "In any event, when we get to the cave we'll find out one way or the other."

Ten yards from the cave, the tracks disappeared completely.

The boys looked at each other.

"Another mystery," Pete said.

They reached the mouth of the cave. It looked empty.

"This opening is almost big enough for a bus," Bob said. "I'll take a look inside and see how far back it goes."

Jupiter peered inside the cave. "All right, Bob. But stay within shouting distance. Pete and I will be with you, as soon as we check the entrance for any clues."

Bob brandished his spearlike weapon and walked into the cave.

"What makes him so brave, all of a sudden?" Pete asked.

Jupiter smiled. "Once we saw the tracks were made by a man-made vehicle, rather than a fantastic creature such as a dragon, I think we all got a lot braver."

He cocked his head, as if listening.

"Perhaps we can tell from the echo of Bob's voice

how large the cave is." He raised his voice. "Just checking, Bob—how are things in there?"

Pete inclined his head, too, in a listening attitude. They heard the sound together. A heavy plopping sound.

Then they heard Bob's voice. It was thin and high-pitched. He spoke only one word but it filled them with terror.

"Help!"

7

A Mysterious Warning

As Jupiter and Pete stared wide-eyed into the dimly lit cave, they heard Bob cry out again.

"Help! Help me!"

"Bob's in trouble!" Pete exclaimed. "Come on!"

Pete, the most muscular and athletic of the trio, darted into the cave. Jupiter tried to keep up with Pete's flying feet.

"Not so fast, Pete," Jupiter said. "He's not too far away, and we have to be careful not to—"

He never completed his sentence. In the gloom of the cave, he suddenly ran into something hard that knocked the wind out of him. He fell to his knees.

Then he heard Pete's voice.

"Stay back, Jupe! I've found him!"

"Where, Pete? I can't see."

Jupiter blinked. Then his eyes adjusted to the darkness of the cave. He saw Pete was on his hands and knees in front of him.

"He's down a hole," Pete said. "I stopped just in time."

"I can't see," Jupiter said. He tried to peer around Pete's shoulder. "Bob," he called. "Where are you?"

Bob's voice was so close, he jumped.

"Down here!" Bob cried. "I fell into some kind of a pit. It seems to be dragging me down!"

"Yipes!" Pete exclaimed. "Quicksand!"

"Impossible," Jupiter said. "Quicksand is usually found in tropical countries."

He wriggled round Pete, carefully feeling the cavern floor with his hands. "I still can't see him. Bob, can you see us?"

"Yes," Bob said. "I'm almost directly under you."

Jupiter leaned over, extending his arm. "Just reach up and grab my hand, Bob. Pete and I will pull you out."

They heard dull plopping sounds below.

"I c-can't!" they heard Bob say after a moment. "Whenever I try, I seem to sink deeper!"

"Push your stick up," Pete suggested. "That broken oar you were holding. Jupe and I could pull you out in a second."

"I can't", Bob said despairingly. "I dropped it when I fell in here."

Pete looked at his piece of driftwood and groaned. "Mine's too light to hold you."

Jupiter was wriggling cautiously round the edge of the pit. "Hang on, Bob," he said. "I'm circling the pit to try to get some idea of its size."

He crawled slowly away.

"Hurry!" Bob cried. "This is no time for measuring things."

"I've got to," Jupiter replied. "It's the only way I can think of to get you out."

He made his way in the darkness on his hands and knees. Bits of earth dropped into the pit, despite his care.

"Watch it!" Bob cried out. "You're starting a landslide!"

"Sorry," Jupiter said. "It's the loose dirt round the edges."

In another moment, he had completely circled the pit and rejoined Pete. "I think we can manage it." He called down to Bob again. "Bob, can you tell us if you are touching bottom?" They heard thrashing sounds below. Then spluttering, spitting noises.

"Not yet," Bob replied testily. "Maybe by the time you geniuses up there think of a way to get me out, I will be."

"If you hold my legs, Jupe, I can reach down for him," Pete said. "We don't have time for anything fancy."

Jupiter shook his head. "I think we can use my plank. Not for pulling him out directly—we'd never get enough leverage on this sandy ground. But the plank is just long enough to reach across the pit and wedge into the sides."

"Then what good is that?" Pete asked. "Bob can't reach that high."

"Yes he can, if we can place it at the right angle," Jupiter said. "I think we can wedge it in from the opposite side."

Pete looked at the thin plank Jupiter held. He nodded, wetting his lips. "It's worth a try. If it will hold his weight."

Jupiter leaned over the ledge. "We'll be trying to reach over your head, Bob," he explained. "It will be up to you to see that the plank is wedged in firmly enough to sustain your weight.

"Because if it slips," he added, "we'll not only lose the plank, but you."

"Thanks a lot," Bob answered. "Only hurry it up. I think I've sunk another couple of inches."

Jupiter left Pete and hurried to the far side. He leaned over the edge and extended the plank.

"I'm pushing it out now," he told his friends. "I don't know if you can see it, Bob. But in a moment it should be passing over your head."

Lying on his stomach, he shoved the plank out foot

by foot. Finally he heard a shout from below.

"I can see it now," Bob called. Then, on a higher despairing note, "I can't reach it. It's too high."

"It's coming down now," Jupiter said. "I'm trying to get the precise angle where it will fit."

He extended the plank a few more inches.

"You're doing fine, Jupe," Bob called. "It's coming in all right. Just another couple of inches."

He waited for Jupiter's next move. Then he heard a scuffling sound. "Come on, Jupe. What's holding you up?"

Jupiter's voice was hoarse. "I'm out too far. I—I'm beginning to fall in myself!"

"Oh, no!" Pete groaned. He leaped to his feet and dashed for the other side.

Jupiter's feet were clawing wildly for purchase on the slippery ground. The rest of him was already tilted downwards over the dark pit. Bits of earth crumbled under his weight and rolled away.

Pete threw himself forward and landed on Jupiter's legs, pinning him there. Then, grabbing Jupiter's belt, he threw his weight backwards.

"Easy, Jupe," he said, panting. "I've got you."

In another moment, he had enough of Jupiter back for the stocky boy to recover his balance.

"Thanks, Pete," Jupiter said breathlessly. "Now if you would just remain over me another few seconds until I get this plank extended all the way—"

They both heard Bob's joyous shout.

"You got it, Jupe!"

"Okay, Bob. Pete and I will now wedge it into the pit at this side. Then it will be up to you to come up it, hand over hand. Can you reach it?"

There was a second's pause. Then, "I got it!"

"All right, Bob," Jupiter said. "Come on, then."

"Roger!" Bob said.

They heard a warning creak. The plank shook under their hands.

"Here he comes!" Pete yelled.

As the plank swayed and shivered under Bob's advancing weight, Jupiter leaned on his end with all his strength.

"It may still break," he whispered to Pete. "Get ready to grab him."

They heard Bob breathing heavily.

"Okay," he panted. "Here I am. Now what?"

Pete leaned over. "Grab my hand, Bob."

Bob's hand shot up quickly. For a brief moment, their grips held together. Then Bob's hand slipped away. He moved frantically to grab the wet plank again.

"He's harder to hold than a greased pig. Jupe," Pete complained. "You want to try it?"

Jupiter shook his head. "I doubt that I'd do it any better than you. We'll have to grab him together."

Bob glared at them from below, as he dangled from the swaying plank. "For Pete's sake, will you guys stop holding these conferences and get me out of here? I'm weighed down with so much mud, I can hardly hold myself up. And my hands are slipping, too—"

Jupe's eyes darted round the interior of the cave. "What we need is a rope," he said. "Something we can throw and loop over him—"

"There's no rope," Pete muttered. "And no time. We're only a couple of inches short. There must be something—"

Suddenly Jupiter's eyes brightened. "I have it!"

His hands went for his belt buckle. Swiftly, he opened it and drew the belt off his waist. Pete watched open-mouthed as Jupiter inserted the end of his belt through the buckle. It made a small loop.

Jupiter let the other end dangle and leaned over the pit again. "I've made a small loop out of my belt, Bob." he said. "When I lower it, let it go over your hand. Your weight will tighten it. Then Pete and I can pull you out."

He slowly let the belt out, lowering it into the pit. Then he braced himself for a tug from below.

"I got it!" Bob yelled. "Pull!"

Jupiter sighed with relief. Pete grinned and reached for his share of the belt. Together, they leaned back and pulled.

Something dark and wet, covered with ooze and slime, slowly came up out of the pit.

8

A Forced Retreat

THE WET FIGURE dropped beside them, panting heavily.

"Thanks, fellows."

"It was Jupe's idea," Pete said. He glanced down ruefully at his own belt. "I'm wearing a belt, too. I just never thought of using it."

"Perhaps that's because you're not as weight conscious as I am," Jupiter said, smiling. "Besides, since my waist is wider than yours, my belt is longer."

Bob wiped mud from his face. "It worked fine, Jupe. I'll never kid you about being overweight again." He glanced down into the pit and drew back, shuddering. "Otherwise I might still be down there."

"All's well that ends well," Pete said. "Now what do we do?"

"We go home," Jupiter said firmly. "Bob's wet and needs a change of clothing. I'm sorry. It was my fault for insisting we investigate the cave without our torches handy."

"It would have been a good idea," Bob agreed. "But I guess it was dumb of me to dash ahead without looking where I was going."

Jupiter stood up, frowning.

"Odd that such a dangerous pit should be so close to the entrance to the cave. I imagine that would keep a lot of curious people out."

"Not if they do things my way," Bob said, grinning weakly. "That would keep a lot of those curious people *in!*"

"Golly," Pete said, a serious note in his voice. "Maybe that's what happened to Mr Allen's dog, and the other missing ones. They might have fallen into that pit, too, and been sucked down."

Jupiter nodded. "It's a possibility. But we were looking for evidence of their tracks before Bob cried for help, and didn't find any."

"Oh?" Pete exclaimed. "Is that what we were doing?" He took a quick look behind him. "Well, let's get out of here while we still can. This place is scary."

In complete agreement, they walked quickly out of the cave.

Jupiter looked back. There were giant boulders on the other side of the cave opening.

"I wonder how far back that cave goes," he said, thoughtfully. "We were told it had been used by smugglers and rum-runners in the past."

"That's right," Pete said. "What about it?"

"The part we were in didn't seem ideal for hiding things. It was too open and easy to get into."

"Maybe there are other passages," Bob said. "Sometimes water erosion wears away the softer rocks. It takes millions of years sometimes. Maybe this area was under water a long time ago. If so, there would be a lot of natural passages."

"Probably," Jupiter agreed, "but we don't have the time to investigate that now. We will have to postpone our search until another time."

"Suits me," Pete said with enthusiasm. "Just as long as we can call it quits for today. I've had it with scares."

"We've all agreed on that," Jupiter said. "The trouble is, we seem to have one more ahead of us."

"What do you mean?" Pete demanded.

Jupiter pointed towards the sea. His companions

looked in that direction. They blinked. It wasn't possible!

Something dark and glittering was rising out of the water.

"I can't make out what it is," Bob whispered.

"It's got a small dark head—like a dragon has, I think," Pete said, shakily.

A large wave came rolling in. It loomed high over the dark shape, then swept over it, covering it completely.

The boys held their ground nervously, peering intently at the swirling water.

The rolling wave crashed and broke on the beach. Another came in after it. Then, as the swirling water eddied back, they saw the dark shape again.

It stood up. It was sleek, black and shining, down to its webbed feet. Slowly it walked ashore.

"Skin diver," Pete said, relieved. "Wearing a face mask and flippers. What a thing to get scared over. Come on. Let's go."

As they turned away, Jupiter spoke softly into their ears. "Red alert! He's carrying a speargun!"

Pete laughed. "So what? He's probably hunting fish or something."

Jupiter shook his head. "He's heading this way."

Suddenly the masked man in the black wetsuit dropped to his knees. He extended his speargun, and then fell prone, aiming it.

"Uh-oh! Look out!" Bob cried. "He's aiming at us!"

"Huh?" Pete said. "Why would he do that?"

He squinted and his face paled. "Excuse me! Bob's right!" He whirled around. "It's got to be us—there's nobody else around!"

Jupiter Jones saw the man lying facing them less

58

than a hundred yards away. The speargun was cradled in his arms and definitely appeared to be pointed at them.

Jupiter had a logical mind. One that worked with almost lightning speed sometimes. He appraised the situation and frowned. It defied all logic.

When logic failed, Jupiter could still depend on a keen sense of preservation. "Red alert," he said. "Scatter and run!"

They whirled instantly and ran for the staircase. As they got closer to it, they saw immediately it was useless. In the excitement, they had forgotten the accident a short while before. They saw the litter of broken steps and railings again. Behind loomed the cliff wall, rising steeply at an angle impossible to climb.

Jupe looked towards the next staircase. It was too far away, requiring a long run over heavy sand that would slow them down. They'd be an easy target on the open beach.

Quickly he made his calculation. "We've got only one chance. Quick! Back into the cave!"

The boys veered off, changed direction and sprinted for the cave opening. They ran desperately, expecting at any moment to hear the sharp retort of the speargun.

Or perhaps to feel the long and deadly steel shaft it propelled.

The sand flew under their feet.

"Almost there!" Jupiter gasped. "Dive!"

The three leaped headlong for the mouth of the cave, almost as one. Then they scurried on hands and knees behind the big boulders for protection.

"Made it!" Pete grunted. "Now what?"

"We hide," Jupiter said, struggling to catch his

breath. "It will give us time—to work out a plan."

"Maybe now's the time to look for those other passages," Bob said.

Jupiter nodded, his cheeks pink with excitement. "Agreed, Bob. But we'll let him make the first move. If he comes this way, then I'll admit our situation demands emergency procedure—such as going deeper into this cave."

Pete was peering over Jupiter's shoulder. His voice was tight. "We'll have to, Jupe—here he comes!"

"Whiskers!" Bob exclaimed. "What'll we do? I don't feel like dropping into that pit again."

Jupiter had backed into the cavern wall.

"Look!" he suddenly called to them.

In the wall, they saw some vertical planking, running up to the ceiling of the cave.

"Jeepers," Pete said. "How did we miss that before?"

"The sand and dust provided a natural covering," Jupiter said. He tapped the panel with his hand. It brought a hollow sound.

"It must be a secret passage," he said. He pushed at the boards. "They appear loose enough to be moved. Take another quick look, Pete. See if that skin diver is still coming for the cave."

Pete peered out and quickly ducked back.

"We've got double trouble," he said, his voice shaking. "Now there are two of them!"

Jupiter frowned. "Two? In that case, we'd better work fast. Help me with these planks."

They tugged and pushed at the planks.

"It's no use," Bob said. "They're wedged in too tightly."

Jupiter shook his head. "There has to be a way." His eyes gleamed suddenly. "Of course! Stupid of me."

The boys held their breath as the divers searched . . .

He kicked at the loose sand under the plank. "All we have to do is dig down a little. Get some of that sand out. That will loosen them up."

Quickly, they dropped to their knees and scooped away at the sand. The wide plank above it suddenly moved.

"That's it," Jupiter said. "Now, if we can turn it enough for us to slip through—"

Once they had disturbed its base, the plank was easy to manage. Bob and Pete went through. Then it was Jupiter's turn.

He struggled to get through the narrow opening. "Can't—do it," he gasped. "Still—too fat!"

Bob and Pete hastily scooped out more sand below, from the other side. The plank swung open, and Jupiter heaved himself through.

"Let's leave a little crack to see through," he whispered.

They swung the heavy board back into place, making sure it didn't fit tightly against its neighbour.

They were still on their knees in the dark pocket of the cavern, when they heard voices.

The first skin diver flicked on a torch.

"I could have sworn those kids ran in here, Harry. Too bad you let that wave knock you down and I had to take my eyes off them."

"We'll find them soon enough, if they're in here," the other answered. "If they're not, we can get to work."

The Three Investigators held their breath as the first man played his torch round the cave. Jupiter, on hands and knees, pressed his face to the opening between the long boards.

Bob and Pete stooped over him, each with an eye at the crack.

The men in the black wetsuits walked ahead. The light faded, as did the sound of their shuffling flippered feet.

The rasping voice of the second man echoed from the pit area. "You must have been imagining it, Jack. Nobody here."

"Guess they got away up the other steps, then."

There was a faint plopping sound and then silence. Jupiter could hear and see nothing more, and drew his face back from the board. Dust and sand were making his nose itch. He wondered if his partners had the same symptoms. A sneeze would be a disaster for them now.

"No sneezing," he whispered. "Cover your noses."

They obeyed his warning, and waited nervously. The cave remained dark and silent. Finally Jupiter stood up.

"They've gone," he whispered. "Let's get out while we can."

They scooped away the loose sand again, and carefully eased back the plank.

"You first this time, Jupe," Pete whispered. "If *you* get through, Bob and I can make it easily."

Jupiter took the suggestion with a smile.

They slipped back into the mouth of the cave and listened. The cave remained silent. They put the board quietly back into place, and brushed in sand until it stood firm again.

Jupiter stood up, his heart beating wildly. He looked at his watch.

"We've had over three hours," he whispered. "Hans will be waiting."

9

Message from a Ghost

"WELL, what do you make of it?" Jupiter asked.

It was an hour after their return with Hans in the truck. Bob was at home getting a much needed shower and change of clothing. Pete and Jupiter were alone in Headquarters.

Pete shrugged. "I can't figure it out. I don't know who those skin divers were, except that their names were Harry and Jack. I don't know why Harry, or Jack, pointed that speargun at us. I don't know why they followed us into the cave. I don't know where they disappeared to or how. I don't even know how we got out of there alive."

Jupiter pinched his lip, and nodded. "Add to that the curious incident of the collapsing staircase, and it's obvious we're confronted with many questions before we try to solve the mystery of Mr Allen's missing dog."

"I've got an idea that will help," Pete said.

"Oh?" Jupiter wheeled round in his chair, his eyes sparkling with interest. "What?"

Pete gestured to the telephone on their desk. "Just pick up that telephone and call Mr Allen. Tell him we've decided not to find his missing dog for him. Tell him we nearly disappeared ourselves. Tell him we're willing to forget the whole thing."

Jupiter ignored the suggestion.

"Our first problem," he stated, "is to determine who

those skin divers were, and what they were doing in the cave."

Pete shook his head. "Why bother with those two tough characters? We were in there, too, and I don't even know what *we* were doing in there."

"Looking for clues of Mr Allen's dragon," Jupiter replied. "And tracks or traces of his Irish setter, Red Rover."

"Well, we didn't find much," Pete declared. "Except that pit. Bob found that for us."

"We found that passage behind the boards," Jupiter said. "It may be a secret tunnel in the cave. Or it could be one of the secret hiding places used by the rum-runners or smugglers in the old days."

"I don't see what that's got to do with us," Pete answered stubbornly. "It wasn't hiding Mr Allen's dog."

Jupiter frowned. "As investigators, we have to return and examine that cave more thoroughly. Don't you realize that?"

Pete nodded reluctantly. "Sure. All I'm wondering about is how those skin divers didn't fall into the pit Bob found? Doesn't that prove they know their way around in there?"

"Maybe, but they did have a torch," Jupiter said. "As to how or why they disappeared, perhaps when we return with torches, we'll discover—"

The telephone rang, for the second time that day.

They stared at it.

It rang again. "Well, answer it," Pete said.

"I will." Jupiter picked it up. "Hello?" he said into the phone. "Hello?"

He held the telephone close to the microphone so that Pete could hear what was said, too. They heard a rasping sound.

"Hello!" Jupe said again. There was no answer.

66

"Maybe it's a wrong number," Pete said.

"I—don't think so," Jupiter said. "Listen!"

They they heard the strange rasping sound again. The sound was like that of somebody trying to breathe, gasping for air with great difficulty.

The curious breathing sounds changed to a voice that seemed to be strangling, as if the speaker had only a few moments of life left.

"Keep—" the strangling voice said. Then, as if it were the most tremendous effort imaginable, the voice continued.

"Away," it said. "Keep . . . away."

Then it became a heavy breathing sound again.

"Keep away from what?" Jupiter asked the telephone.

"My . . . cave," the voice said. There was another long gasping sound and then silence.

"Why?" Jupiter asked. "Say, who is this?"

The voice sounded hollow now. "Dead . . . men," it said slowly, "tell . . . no . . . tales!"

There was a long trembling gasp, and then silence.

Jupiter hung up. For a moment, he and Pete sat staring at the phone. Then Pete hopped up.

"I just remembered we're having dinner early tonight," he said. "I'd better get on home."

Jupiter jumped up. "I'll leave, too. Aunt Mathilda might want me to clean up the yard a little."

Quickly both boys bolted from the trailer.

They hadn't had any trouble understanding what the ghostly voice had told them. It was a very simple message.

Keep away from my cave!
Dead men tell no tales!

Old Mr Allen had told them about a dragon entering a cave.

He hadn't mentioned a dead man—or a ghost!

10

The Death of Seaside

MEANWHILE, Bob had showered and changed his clothes. By the time he reached the Rocky Beach Public Library, where he had a part-time job, he felt more cheerful.

As he walked in, Miss Bennett, the librarian, looked up and smiled.

"Oh, Bob," she said, "I'm really glad to see you today. It's been one of those busy days. So many visitors, and now, of course, so many books to put back on the shelves. Could you get right to it?"

"Sure," Bob replied.

He picked up the sizable stack of returnable books and put them away one by one. Then he turned to the reading-room tables. A lot of books had been left out, and he gathered them up. The title of the one on top was *Legends of California*. He flipped the pages idly and saw one chapter entitled "Seaside: Dream of a City That Died".

"Hmmm," Bob said to himself. "That might be interesting."

He put it aside thoughtfully. This was a lucky find. Anxious to return to the book when he had finished his duties at the library, Bob attacked the stacks of books lying about with record speed.

When he had finished putting them all back on the shelves, Miss Bennett asked him to mend some books with torn bindings. He took them into the back

68

storage room and secured the covers with plastic tape. In a little while, he had done everything that had to be done.

He returned to Miss Bennett's desk.

"Everything's in order, Miss Bennett. I have some research to do now, if there isn't anything else you need me to do—"

Miss Bennett shook her head, and Bob hurried to the reading table with the book of Californian legends. He didn't know very much about Seaside at all, he realized. Neither Jupiter nor Pete knew much about it either. Certainly none of them had ever heard a word about the town *dying!*

Quickly he opened the book to the chapter about Seaside. It started with these words:

There are cities which are plagued by ill fortune, just as people. Seaside's dreams of becoming a key resort community went up in smoke fifty years ago.

The bright and bustling city its planners had visualized and gambled their fortunes on, was never to be. The elaborate canals and waterways, constructed to remind visitors of Venice, have crumbled and been replaced with factories. The once elegant hotels have been boarded up or bull-dozed to make way for motorway construction going north and south.

Perhaps Seaside's most bitter disappointment was the failure of its underground railway, the first on the West Coast. Investors, as well as the public, were cool about plans for a rapid transport system linking the coastal part of Seaside with the business section and other nearby communities. As a result, the underground network was never completed, and its few miles of tunnel remain boarded up and forgotten, a ghostly secret and costly reminder of the city that died before it had a chance to grow up.

"Wow!" Bob said to himself. The town of Seaside meant more to him now. It was more than fifty years since it had died—the book he was reading was several years old. If he hadn't found it by accident, he probably never would have known the story of the place they had visited.

He wrote down some of the main facts about Seaside and put the book away. Then he sat thinking. He had a great deal to tell Jupiter, but he decided to wait until after dinner. It was almost that time now and he was hungry.

He said goodbye to Miss Bennett and cycled home. His mother was preparing dinner, and his father was reading his newspaper and smoking his pipe. He greeted Bob with a smile.

"Hi, son," he said. "I understand you came home with enough mud on you to test our washing machine to the limit of the manufacturer's most exaggerated claims."

"Right, Dad," Bob said. "I fell into a hole. At first I thought it was quicksand, but it turned out to be mostly mud and water."

"Quicksand? Nothing like that round here, to my knowledge."

"Not Rocky Beach," Bob said. "It was at Seaside. We're on a case that took us down there. We were investigating one of the caves."

His father nodded, and put his paper down. "In the old days it would have been worth your life to stick your nose into one of them. A lot of the caves around Haggity's Point there were used by rum-runners, and before that by pirates."

"So I heard," Bob said. "And I just came across a book in the library that told all about how Seaside was a city that died before it grew up. Did you know that?"

His father was a newspaperman who always seemed to have a secret store of knowledge. He nodded again.

"A lot of people lost their shirts and went broke when they guessed wrong about that town. After the big fire at the amusement park, its luck turned bad."

"It didn't look that bad to me," Bob said. "It's as big as Rocky Beach here."

Mr Andrews smiled. "Since then, they've had fifty-odd years to rebuild and it's a bustling, thriving city now. But not what it was intended to be, a big resort. Now it's just another place to live and make money."

"Tough," Bob said. "I read they even started their own underground railway but never got round to finishing it."

Mr Andrews leaned forward. "That particular decision cost one of the early Seaside planners his life. He committed suicide after losing his personal fortune pledged to the building of the underground system." He frowned, and puffed on his pipe. "His name escapes me now, but he was the big man with the big dream. If enough people had shared his conviction and enthusiasm, Seaside might have become what he wanted—the biggest Fun City of them all."

Mrs Andrews' voice interrupted, clear and firm.

"Dinner's ready."

Bob wanted to hear more but his father got up and went to the table. Bob followed and sat down. There was a lot Jupiter should know.

71

"I say we forget all about finding Mr Allen's lost dog," Pete was saying firmly. "It may be only a missing pet to him, but to me it's also a dragon, and two nasty-looking skin divers with loaded spearguns who don't like kids. Not to mention that mud hole that sucks in people, and the staircase that falls apart when you run down it. Plus whatever it was that called on the telephone warning us to keep away from its cave. That sounds like good advice to me, especially coming from a dead man!"

Bob's eyes widened. "What's *that* all about?"

It was an hour after dinner, and the boys had met again in Headquarters to discuss their plans.

"After you went home to change, Bob," Jupiter explained, "we received a mysterious telephone call." He told Bob about it, repeating the message word for word.

"Sounds like a gag to me," Bob said, at last. He licked his lips. "If it's not, somebody is telling us we're not wanted near that cave."

Jupe's face had a familiar stubborn look. "We haven't seen anything of the mysterious dragon yet," he said. "I suggest we go back tonight for another look."

"Let's vote on it," Pete suggested hastily. "My vote is we abandon the case now. All in favour say aye!"

"Aye! Aye! Aye!" The word was repeated shrilly by Blackbeard, the trained mynah bird whose cage hung near the desk in Headquarters.

"Quiet, you!" Pete snapped. "You're not a paid-up member of this club. We only allow you to live here!"

"Dead men tell no tales!" Blackbeard called out and laughed shrilly.

Bob turned to Jupiter. "Maybe that's who you heard —Blackbeard."

Jupiter shook his head. "No, Bob. It came from somebody who seemed to have trouble breathing and speaking. If it was done deliberately to create the effect of a dying man—or even a ghost—it succeeded. It was actually scary, wasn't it, Pete?"

Pete shrugged. "No more than anything else that's happened so far." He pushed back his hair. "If I'm not grey yet, maybe I will be by tomorrow."

Jupiter grinned. "You're no more scared than any of us, Pete. You're just putting on an act."

"Want to bet?" Pete said.

Jupiter's answer was to pick up the phone.

"I'm betting that when Worthington shows up for us in the Rolls-Royce, you'll want to come along," he said.

Less than an hour later, Pete looked out of the window of the smooth-riding, gold-plated, luxuriously appointed old car. It purred almost silently along the Pacific Coast Highway heading for the outskirts of Seaside. Worthington, the tall and polite English chauffeur, was at the wheel, driving with his usual skill.

"Sometimes I wish you'd never won the use of this car in that contest, Jupe," Pete complained. "When I think of all the trouble it's got us into."

"*Out* of, too, Pete," Bob reminded him. "And when our first thirty days' use of it was up, you weren't too happy about it, either, as I recall."

An English boy they had helped at that critical time had made the necessary financial arrangements for the continued use of the car. The Three Investigators had almost unlimited access to the Rolls-Royce, as well as the services of its driver, Worthington.

Pete leaned back against the leather upholstery and

smiled. "I've got to admit this beats riding in the truck, not to mention walking."

Jupiter had given the directions needed to get them off the highway and on to the narrow ridge road overlooking the beach at Seaside. Now he leaned forward and tapped the chauffeur's shoulder.

"This will do fine, Worthington," he said. "Wait for us here."

"Very good, Master Jones," the chauffeur replied. The big Rolls-Royce with the huge old headlights shining into the night eased up to the side of the road.

The boys tumbled out. Jupiter reached back into the car for their equipment.

"Torches, a camera and tape recorder," he said. "Now we'll be prepared for any emergency, and be able to document it, as well."

He handed Bob the recorder. "For recording any sounds of dragon, Bob, or ghosts who have trouble breathing and talking."

Pete took one of the three powerful torches. Jupe put a coil of rope on his other arm.

"What's the rope for?" Pete asked.

"It always pays to be prepared," Jupiter told him. "It's a hundred feet of light nylon. It should hold us if the other staircases have been tampered with and we have to get down from the cliff by our own means."

They walked a little way along the quiet, dark street. Jupiter led the way to the staircase he had chosen for their descent. It was several hundred yards from the one that had collapsed under their weight that morning.

His companions joined him on the ridge and looked down. The beach appeared deserted. The rising moon cast a dim glow through light clouds. The soft hiss of

74

the waves lapping the sand below was periodically drowned out by the roar of the breakers that loomed up dark and menacing beyond.

Pete licked his lips nervously, grasped the handrail of the old staircase, and stood still for a moment listening. Bob and Jupe listened, too.

All they could hear was the dull roar of the surf and the beating of their hearts.

"Well, good luck one and all," Pete said tightly.

As the boys took the first step down, they felt certain they heard the ocean roar a little louder, as if in anticipation!

II

Terror in the Night

THE STAIRS were dark and the salty night wind stung their faces. The towering cliff wall jutted towards the ocean, casting long, gloomy shadows on the moonlit sand.

The staircase held their weight, and they ran down the last few steps with more confidence, jumping off to the sand with relieved sighs.

Jupiter looked up. Only an occasional light was burning in the houses along the ridge.

They trudged along the damp dark sand and passed the old staircase that had collapsed under them earlier.

As they approached the cave entrance, they came to a halt, listening intently and looking about carefully. No one, as far as they could detect, was moving inside or anywhere about.

Jupe looked up. The cliff wall jutted out blocking his view of the ridge. He scowled, feeling this was important somehow, but not sure why.

At last he nodded. "All clear." They slipped quickly inside and again Jupiter paused to listen. Pete was puzzled. Jupe was acting as if they were on a commando raid.

"Why the big act?" Pete whispered. "I thought this wasn't supposed to be so dangerous."

"It never pays to be careless," Jupe whispered back.

Pete flicked his torch on and let the light play on the walls of the cave. Then he lowered it to the ground ahead. He gasped in surprise.

"Do you see what I see?" he demanded. "The cave ends right there—just behind the pit. How did those two skin divers get out?"

Jupiter walked forward slowly and flashed his light around.

"It's a smaller cave than I expected," he said thoughtfully. "And that's a good question, Pete. How did those skin divers leave? And where did they disappear to?"

They walked about and tested the cave walls.

"Solid," Pete said. "That's great!"

"What do you mean, Pete?" Bob asked.

"Don't you get it?" Pete answered. "Look how small this cave is! And that pit is pretty small, too. What I mean is, no dragon could ever fit in here!"

Jupe looked puzzled. "And yet Mr Allen said he saw a dragon come out of the sea and enter this cave under the cliff." He looked intently down at the pit. "Those skin divers didn't just vanish into thin air. We'll have to assume there's another cave entrance here somewhere. Or another opening somewhere in this cave. There may be other, larger passages running close by."

"Wow!" Bob suddenly exclaimed. "I just remembered something!"

Quickly he told his companions what he had read in the library and heard from his father.

Jupiter's eyes were thoughtful. "A tunnel, you say?"

Bob nodded excitedly. "It was supposed to be the first underground railway system on the West Coast. It was never all finished, but part of it was, and still exists. Sort of like a ghost railway."

"That's interesting, Bob," Jupe said. "But that tunnel could be miles away. And we don't know that whoever started the tunnel came this far with it, or started at this end."

Bob looked deflated. "I guess you're right, Jupe."

"We'll look for it while we're here," Jupiter said. "But the best way to find the tunnel would be from a map. We could probably get one at the Seaside City Planning Board offices."

"After over fifty years?" Pete laughed. "Whoever drew up that map probably died a long time ago. And if the map is still around, my bet is it's buried somewhere under a lot of old papers and dust."

Jupiter nodded. "Could be, Pete. But as long as we're here tonight, we might look for the tunnel while we continue our investigation.

"I was thinking of that little passage we found this morning behind the boards. That should be safe enough to start with, I imagine."

Pete and Bob nodded in agreement and moved over to the boarded section. Jupe brushed some of the sand and dirt away from it, exposing a large board. As he did so, Bob saw Jupe's eyes suddenly gleam with excitement.

"What is it, Jupe?" Bob whispered.

Jupe was looking puzzled.

"I'm not quite sure yet," he said. "It looks like plywood."

"Plywood?" Bob repeated.

"I believe so," Jupe said, feeling the board. "But I'm not certain yet as to how it relates to this mystery. Just now we'd better go ahead with getting some of the sand away so we can move these boards."

Soon the plank they had moved before was loose enough. They got it out of the way, slipped through the narrow opening, then carefully replaced it. Then they flicked on their torches to see where they were.

They were in a small, narrow cave. The ceiling was low, leaving them just enough room to stand without stooping. It was damp and sloped abruptly to a low shelf of rock in the rear.

"Another dead end," Pete muttered. "It doesn't lead anywhere."

Jupiter shrugged. "However, it does make an ideal hiding place for smugglers or pirates. I imagine it's been used a lot in the past. The old planks indicate they they tried to keep it a secret place."

Bob flashed his light on the cave floor. "Pirates, eh? Maybe they left us a few gold doubloons."

He and Pete dropped to their hands and knees and felt carefully in the thin film of sand for treasure.

Pete was the first to give up. "Nothing," he said, disappointed. "If they ever did use it to hide their loot, they sure were careful about picking it all up when they left."

Bob kept searching on hands and knees until he reached the far end of the cave. "Maybe they swept some of it into the corner," he whispered.

Jupiter was flashing his light at the boarded-up section. He scraped some of the dust and sand off the boards and was examining them when he heard Bob cry out.

"What's up, Bob?" Jupe asked.

He heard a rumbling sound. Jupiter turned and stared.

Bob had disappeared.

"Bob!" Jupiter stepped towards the other side of the cave and then stopped in his tracks, dumbfounded.

"What happened?" Pete asked. He was on his feet, staring.

Jupiter could only point to the cave wall they were facing. "He was here a second ago. Didn't you see him? Then the wall seemed to swallow him up."

"What?" Pete leaped headlong for the wall. It

brought him up short. "I don't get it," he muttered, shining his torch on the floor. "There's no pit this time."

As he stooped to examine the floor of the cave, there was a rumbling noise. Pete's eyes widened and he gripped his heavy torch tighter. He looked up at Jupiter and was surprised to see the stocky boy smile.

"It's okay," Jupe said. "He's coming back now."

Pete whirled in time to see the movement in the wall. A small section was turning. The next moment there was a gaping hole where there had been a wall, and Bob was on his knees crawling through.

"How about that!" Bob exclaimed. "Whiskers! A secret moving rock panel. I just happened to lean on it and—wham! It opened!"

"What's on the other side?" Jupe asked excitedly.

Bob's jaw dropped. "I didn't get a chance to notice, Jupe. It happened too fast. Let's see if I can open it again."

He backed against the low cave wall, squatting. Nothing happened at first, and he shifted his shoulders. Suddenly, they heard a sharp clicking sound. Then the rock rumbled and Bob tilted back.

"Here I go again," he cried. "Better use it while it's open!"

He tumbled through the opening, and then Pete and Jupe slid through.

"Wow!" Pete exclaimed. "This is more like it!"

This cave was very wide and high. It extended back as far as their torches could reach, running inland parallel to the first cave they had entered.

The Three Investigators jumped to their feet to examine it.

As they did, they heard a slight rumbling noise behind them. They whirled, too late.

The secret rock opening had closed behind them!

"Uh-oh!" Pete muttered. "That does it!"

"That's what happened to Bob before. I'm sure we'll be able to work out how it works later," Jupe said. "Probably a simple leverage system. Let's forget it now while we investigate this cave."

Bob looked up at the high vaulted ceiling.

"Wow!" he gasped. "Look at the size of it, Jupe! This might be the tunnel I read about!"

Jupiter nodded. "Possibly, Bob. But if you notice, the walls and ceiling are rough, unfinished rock, as any cave is. The tunnel you told us about was completed. It would be in a more finished condition, with concrete walls possibly and a paved flooring. Perhaps tracks, too. Or the bedding for them."

He shook his head, and flashed his light about. "No, this looks like any large natural cave. There's no entrance to the beach and water behind us, either. The walls appear solid all the way round. But let's follow its course under the cliff. It may still lead us to the old underground railway tunnel you mentioned."

"What I like about it," Pete said, "is that there's no way out to the beach. That means, there's no way in for things like dragons!"

"Which means we're in luck," Jupiter said smiling. "There's one thing certain about this cave anyway. It happens to be large enough to contain a dragon or any other creature that size."

"Thanks for reminding me," Pete muttered. "I nearly felt good there for about half a second."

The cave floor was fairly smooth and level and they advanced along it steadily. Then they stopped short.

The passage ended suddenly in a high, vertical grey wall.

"End of the road," Pete said. "Looks like all we've

discovered is the world's biggest unused parking lot!"

Jupiter was pinching his lower lip and looking puzzled.

"What's wrong, Jupe?" Bob asked.

"That wall ahead of us," Jupe said. "There's something about it that doesn't look quite right."

Bob and Pete flashed their lights on it, and shook their heads.

"It looks like a wall to me," Bob said. "Naturally I'm as disappointed as you are. I wanted—"

Jupiter had his eyes half closed and wasn't listening. He peered closely at the wall and tapped it. Then he hit other parts of it, his ear close to the grey surface.

"It sounds funny, Jupe," Bob said.

Jupiter nodded, frowning, then walked to the side of the cave and tapped the wall there.

"There's a difference," he said finally. "I can't explain it exactly but—"

"Oh, come on, Jupe," Pete interrupted impatiently. "If you can't prove it's not a wall, then it is. Let's get out of here. I'm getting cold."

Jupiter's face lit up. "That's it!" he exclaimed. "Cold! The wall isn't cold. But the sides of the cave are. Feel the difference for yourselves."

Bob and Pete hastily compared the feeling of the wall and the sides of the cave.

"You're right," Pete admitted. "It's not as cold as the sides of the cave. But what does that prove? Don't forget it's under some of those houses along the ridge. Maybe heat comes down from them and warms the wall a little."

"Heat rises, Pete," Jupe said.

"There may be another pocket or passage inside," Bob suggested. "That could warm it, too, Jupe."

82

Jupiter shook his head, his mouth forming the stubborn line they were accustomed to seeing when he disagreed with them.

He took out his pocket knife and started to scrape at the rough grey slab.

Pete laughed. "You'll only ruin your blade trying to cut through that rock, Jupe. What you need is a small stick of dynamite."

Jupiter ignored Pete's remark and continued scraping away at the wall surfaces. He looked at his blade and saw lumpy grey particles clinging to it.

He turned to face his companions. His mouth was open with a triumphant smile as if he had something important to reveal. But as he looked over their shoulders, his smile faded.

"The cave," he said hoarsely. "I d-don't know how— but it's opening behind you!"

His companions whirled in disbelief. There had been no opening before. How could it be opening now?

They watched, with staring eyes, what had to be impossible!

The cave opened wider, slowly. It became somewhat lighter. They felt a breeze.

They stood staring, their hearts pounding wildly, as it continued to open. They could dimly see the sand now, and farther out, the darker line of the ocean.

Jupiter was the first to speak.

"Quick! We've got to get back into that smaller cave!"

The Three Investigators ran forward and threw themselves at the small rock that had opened for them before.

Bob pressed at it frantically with his hands. He hit

it with his shoulder. Then he looked at his companions, his voice shaking.

"I—I forgot how I did it before. I can't open it!"

"Impossible," Jupe grunted. "It was just a matter of leverage. We can find the spot."

He joined Pete in pressing and pounding the resisting rock, while Bob continued his own search for the pressure point he had found earlier.

Light suddenly flooded the cavern, and they froze. The cave opening was widening. And something was moving towards them. Something huge and dark from the sea!

Pete gripped Jupe's shoulder. "Am I seeing things?" he gasped.

Jupiter, stunned, shook his head. His mouth was very dry and his eyes blinked rapidly. "No—" Jupe replied hoarsely "—it's a dragon, all right!"

The monstrous serpentine shape came closer and they could see water glistening on its dark wet skin. The shadowy head was small and triangular, held high on a long, swaying curved neck. Its yellow eyes were fixed on the cave, and bored into them like twin headlights. It advanced, making a strange humming sound.

In another moment, it was close enough to block the cave opening. Its head dipped low and the boys saw its long forked tongue flick in and out, as if getting ready to taste them. It hissed. Its hum was like a longing sigh.

Frantically, they continued their efforts to escape from the cave, hitting and throwing their weight against the rock from every possible angle.

"A-a-a-agh!" The monster was entering the cave now and they could hear its rasping breath.

They cringed back against the rock as the terrifying

The monster loomed darkly above the terrified trio!

dragon loomed high above them. Then the long curving neck swung round and the dark head with its great staring yellow eyes lowered.

The long wet jaws opened and they saw its teeth, incredibly large and shining. It breathed again in its harsh rasping manner, and then it coughed and stopped.

Jupiter had read of the warning cough of the great jungle tiger as it prowled for prey. But he had never thought much about it. He remembered it now and shuddered.

His eyes were riveted on the dark head of the monster. It swayed back and forth hypnotically. Then, suddenly, it dipped closer towards them. Jupiter shrank back against his companions, his hands still frantically searching for the trigger point of the stubborn, un-yielding rock behind him.

The dragon's wet jaws loomed closer. Now they opened again and the frightened boys felt its hot steaming breath.

Suddenly the rock behind them clicked and trembled. Jupiter turned as it opened and saw Bob fall through. Pete sat frozen, staring helplessly up at the dragon. Jupiter jerked his arm and shoved him through after Bob. Then, holding his breath, he hurled himself through the narrow opening.

The rock rumbled shut, and the boys sighed their relief. But it was short-lived.

They heard the muffled, angry roar of the dragon. Then they felt the rock tremble as something heavy clawed and pounded at it from the other side.

12

The Grip of Fear

"It's coming after us!" Pete cried.

The roaring noise from the other passage grew louder. The rock that linked the two caves trembled under the pounding. Sand and small rocks started to fall from the roof of the small cave they were huddled in. The air became clouded with dry, gritty dust.

"Landslide!" Pete said, coughing.

"We're trapped!" Bob cried. "We'll suffocate!"

Jupiter remembered what they had been told about the cave—the danger of landslides, of being buried alive.

It appeared Arthur Shelby had not been joking.

More rocks fell. The pounding and roaring seemed to grow in intensity. Jupe shook his head, trying to get rid of his helpless creeping terror.

Dazed and frightened, he found his eyes fixed on the planks at the other end of their cave. Of course! It was incredible how fear fogged one's mind.

"The planks!" he yelled. "We go out the same way we got in!"

The three frightened investigators leaped for the boards. Jupe and Bob scooped desperately at the loose sand at the bottom, while Pete stood pounding at the thick board, trying to move it. In another moment that seemed like a lifetime, it was free. They squirmed through.

They swung the big board back and hastily kicked

sand underneath it, wedging it in place. Then they looked at each other, panting.

Jupe's head bobbed.

"Now we run for it!" he said.

Jupiter didn't intend to lead the way. His feet did it for him. They took him straight out of the mouth of the cave. Then he was on the sand, running.

Right beside him was Pete. Pete was the best athlete of the trio, and the fastest runner. Bob was next. Ordinarily neither of them would have had any trouble passing Jupiter.

Their torches made erratic bobbing paths of light as they ran. They passed the broken staircase. Finally, they were at the steps of the second staircase that ran to the top of the ridge. Worthington was up there, they knew, and the powerful Rolls-Royce that could whisk them to safety. Behind them was the roaring creature that had come out of the sea, and was angrily looking for them.

They were halfway up and still there was nothing behind to snatch at them with cruel jaws and hot steaming breath. Then they were on the top, panting and gasping for breath.

Ahead of them, far in the distance, were the twinkling lights of Los Angeles. And parked down the street, was the waiting car with Worthington at the wheel.

They raced to the big, sleek Rolls-Royce, its metal parts and golden door handles gleaming in the moonlight. The door was flung open, and they piled into the rear seat.

"Worthington!" Jupiter panted. "Take us home."

"Very good, Master Jones," the tall, dignified chauffeur replied, and the big car came purring to life. It picked up speed and began its long sweeping turn down to the Pacific Coast Highway, going faster and faster.

"I didn't know you could run so fast, Jupe," gasped Pete.

"Neither did I," Jupe replied through puffed cheeks. "Maybe—it's because—I never saw—a dragon before."

"Whiskers!" Bob exclaimed, as he leaned back against the leather-cushioned seat. "Am I glad we've got the use of this car!"

"That goes double for me," Pete said. "But how do you figure that dragon showing up, after we had decided there couldn't be any such thing?"

"I don't know," Jupiter said, puffing as he tried to regain his breath.

"Well, if you ever find out, don't tell me," Pete said. "I'll have enough trouble forgetting that I saw it tonight!"

"How could it happen?" Bob asked. "According to all the books I've read, dragons are supposed to be extinct. There just aren't such things around to-day."

Jupiter shook his head.

"I don't know," He frowned and pinched at his lower lip. "The obvious answer would be that we didn't see one. If there aren't any, then we couldn't possibly have seen one."

"Are you kidding?" Pete demanded. "If we didn't see one, then what was that thing that came into the cave breathing hot steam at us?"

"It sure looked like a dragon," Bob said.

Worthington turned his head. "I beg your pardon, young gentlemen, but I couldn't help overhearing. Do I understand you correctly, that you saw a dragon this evening? A real live one?"

"We sure did, Worthington," Pete said. "It came out of the sea and headed straight for a cave we were investigating. Did you ever see one?"

The chauffeur shook his head. "No, I can't say that I've been that fortunate. But in Scotland, they had something equally terrifying that a few people were privileged to see. A long undulating sea serpent. It was called the Loch Ness monster and it still appears, I'm told, from time to time."

"Did you ever see it, Worthington?" Jupe asked.

"No, Master Jones," the chauffeur replied. "But when I was a lad, I travelled near the loch—as their lakes are called—and word would spread rapidly when it was sighted. I consider it one of the major disappointments of my life that I have never seen the Loch Ness monster. It was reputed to be at least a hundred feet long."

"Mmmm." Jupiter thought about it. "And you've never seen a dragon, either, you said."

"Not a real one," Worthington said, smiling. "Only the kind they use before the football game."

"Football game?" Bob asked.

The dignified chauffeur nodded. "That annual New Year's pageant you people have near here in Pasadena. The big floats of flowers. The Rose Bowl parade, I believe it's called."

"Well, the one we saw a little while ago wasn't made out of flowers," Pete said quickly. "I can tell you that. Right, Jupe?"

"Mmm," Jupe replied. "Definitely not made out of flowers. It was a real dragon, all right," He hesitated. "At least we're all agreed it *looked* like one."

"I'm glad you agree for once," Pete said.

Jupiter scowled. He was pinching his lower lip between his thumb and forefinger, always a sign he was in deep thought. He looked out of the window of the speeding car and continued to pinch his lip without replying.

When the Rolls-Royce reached the Jones Salvage Yard, Jupiter thanked Worthington and said he would call again the next time they needed transportation.

"Very good, Master Jones," Worthington said. "I must say I enjoyed the assignment this evening. It's a welcome change from driving wealthy old ladies and well-to-do businessmen. Before parting, however, I hope you don't mind answering one question that comes to mind. About your dragon, if I may."

"Sure, Worthington. What about it?"

"Well, sir," the chauffeur said, "one might say you were privileged this evening to see a real live dragon, in the flesh, so to speak. At close quarters, might I ask?"

"Too close," Pete answered abruptly. "It was practically right on top of us."

"Good," the chauffeur said, his usual reserved manner dissolved. "Then perhaps you gentlemen took notice. Is it true, as the legend would have it, that the monster breathes out smoke and fire?"

Jupiter thought and shook his head slowly. "No, Worthington. This one didn't. At least, all we saw was the smoke."

"Ah!" Worthington said. "A pity. I should have been most pleased if you had witnessed the total effect."

"Maybe *you* would, Worthington," Pete said. "But what we saw was enough, believe me. I've had enough effect to last me a lifetime. Just talking about it gives me goose-pimples."

The chauffeur nodded and drove off. Jupiter led his partners into the junkyard. His Uncle Titus and Aunt Mathilda were already asleep inside the little house that adjoined the yard. There was just a dim nightlight on for Jupiter.

Jupiter turned to Pete and Bob. "I don't know if

you'll like this, but we will have to return to the cave, dragon or not."

"What?" Pete howled. "Don't you realize we're lucky just to be back here alive?"

Jupe nodded. He held his arms up and showed his empty hands. "My torch is still in my belt, just like yours and Bob's. But in our panic when we ran out of the cave, we forgot all our equipment. My camera, the recorder, the rope. That's one reason for our going back there."

"Okay," Pete said grudgingly. "That makes a little sense, but not too much. What's your other reason?"

"The dragon itself," Jupiter said slowly. "I don't believe it was real!"

His partners stared at him.

"Not real?" Pete demanded. "Are you trying to tell us that thing that frightened us out of our wits wasn't *real*?"

Jupiter nodded.

Bob shook his head. "If that wasn't a real live dragon, I'll eat my shirt."

"I admit it looked like one," Jupe said.

Pete looked annoyed. "Then what are you talking about?"

"I admit the dragon looked like one," Jupe repeated. "But it didn't *act* like one!

"It's too late now to discuss it," Jupe said. "I'll give you my reasons for not believing that was a real live dragon tomorrow morning. And, if I'm proved wrong next time we visit the cave, I'll do as *you* threatened, Bob—I'll eat *my* shirt."

"You won't have to bother," Pete said. "The dragon will eat it for you. And whatever else is handy."

13

Jest of the Joker

BOB had trouble sleeping. Tired as he was from the harrowing events at the cave in Seaside, he had no sooner closed his eyes than he was being pursued from cave to cave by a monstrous dragon breathing hot steam at him. At last he managed to fall soundly asleep, only to be wakened by his mother calling him for breakfast.

His father was finishing his breakfast when Bob came to the table. He nodded to Bob, then glanced at his watch.

"Good morning, son. Did you have a good time with your friends last night?"

"Yes, Dad," Bob answered. "Kind of."

His father stood up, dropping his napkin on the table. "That's fine. By the way, I don't know if it's important, but you seemed interested in the Seaside tunnel yesterday, and after you left, I happened to recall the name of the man who had lost his fortune building it."

"Oh?" Bob asked. "Who was it, Dad?"

"Labron Carter."

"Carter?" Bob instantly thought of the Mr Carter they had met. The one with the bad temper and big shotgun.

"Yes. He lost his vigorous health, too, once the Seaside Town Council turned away from his plans to make Seaside the resort city he had envisaged. The combination of losing his health, fortune and reputation was too much for him—he killed himself."

"That's too bad. Did he have a family?"

Mr Andrews nodded. "His wife died shortly afterwards. His son is the sole survivor." Mr Andrews looked thoughtful for a moment. "That is, if he is still alive," he added. "Remember this all happened over fifty years ago."

Bob waved goodbye as his father left for the newspaper office where he worked. He added this latest information to his notes. He wondered what Jupe would say when he presented his own evidence. Proof that somebody was still alive who knew about the original tunnel. Somebody with a grudge to bear against the city that had broken his father's heart. Somebody who had a very nasty disposition.

Bob couldn't imagine how the present Mr Carter might try to get even. He put his notes in his pocket, finished his breakfast and hurriedly left.

Perhaps Jupe would be able to tie things up later at the Jones Salvage Yard.

"Golly," Pete Crenshaw said, an apprehensive note in his voice. "What Bob's told us about the Carter family sure makes sense, Jupe. More than your remark about the dragon being fake," he added.

The Three Investigators were gathered together again at Headquarters. Bob had started the meeting by reading his notes, as usual, and had first mentioned Labron Carter. But he had even more surprises for his friends.

"I remembered what you said last night about the dragon," Bob said. "And I went straight from my house to the library this morning and did a lot of research before our meeting."

Jupiter glanced at the papers in Bob's hand.

"I believe it would be most constructive to our meeting this morning, Bob, if you came directly to the point," Jupe said. "To wit, are there dragons living today, or not?"

Bob shook his head. "Not. No dragons. Not a single book gave any evidence of dragons living today."

"That's crazy!" Pete exploded. "Those guys just don't know where to look. If they spent a little time around a certain cave in Seaside at night, they'd find one, all right. A nice big one!"

Jupe held up his hands. "I suggest we listen while Bob reads his report. Then we'll discuss it. Continue, Bob."

Bob looked down at his notes. "The closest thing I found to a dragon is a huge lizard called the Dragon of Komodo. It's large for a lizard—grows up to ten feet long—but nowhere near as big as the dragon we saw."

"Maybe one of them got some extra vitamins," said Pete. "Maybe that's our dragon."

"No," said Bob. "The Dragon of Komodo doesn't breathe smoke, and it only lives on one small island in the East Indies. And it doesn't look much like that creature in the cave. I think we can safely say there are no dragons living today.

"But I did find a lot of living creatures that attack, kill and even *eat* man!" He glanced at his companions. "Do you want me to continue?"

Jupe nodded. "Certainly. We must know our natural enemies—as well as the ones intending to fool us by pretending to be natural. Read your list, Bob."

"Here goes," Bob said. "One million people killed each year by disease-carrying insects; forty thousand die of snakebite; two thousand from tigers; one thousand are eaten by crocodiles, and another thousand are food for sharks." He looked up.

"Notice if you will, Pete," Jupe said, "no mention so far of any statistics covering the incidence of dragons and humans. Continue, Records."

"Those are the big numbers," Bob said. "There are also a lot caused by elephant, hippo, rhino, wolf, lion, hyena and leopard. Some of these are accidents. There are man-killers and man-eaters. A lot are intentional 'rogue' killers.

"But according to this book—*Man Is the Prey* by James Clarke—the dangers from some beasts are greatly exaggerated. Like polar bears, pumas, eagles and alligators. He said tarantulas are absolutely harmless, that grizzly bears do very little real damage, and that the apes have enough intelligence to stay away from man. Also that the most likely places you can go if you want to be eaten are central Africa and the Indian subcontinent. The safest place, he says, is Ireland, with nothing there more dangerous than the bumblebee!"

Bob folded his notes. There was silence in the little room.

"Any comment?" Jupe asked Pete.

Pete shook his head. "Seaside sounds pretty safe after that," he said smiling. "All you have to do now is convince me that dragon last night wasn't real."

"Well, to begin with," Jupe said. "We didn't see—" He was interrupted by the telephone ringing.

Jupe reached for it, and then hesitated.

"Go ahead. Pick it up," Pete said. "It might be another call from that dead guy—or ghost. He probably tried to tell that dragon to keep out of his cave, too."

Jupiter smiled and picked the telephone up. "Hello?" he said.

As usual, he held the telephone close to the microphone so Bob and Pete could hear the conversation.

"Hello," said a familiar voice. "Alfred Hitchcock here. Is that young Jupiter?"

"Yes. Hello, Mr Hitchcock. I suppose you're calling to find out how we're doing with our investigation for your friend?"

"Yes," the hearty voice replied. "I had assured Allen you boys would clear up the mystery of his missing dog with dispatch and ingenuity. I'm calling now to verify my own assurances. Have you found the dog yet?"

"Not yet, Mr Hitchcock," Jupe said. "We've got another mystery to solve first. A mystery of a coughing dragon."

"A coughing dragon?" Mr Hitchcock repeated. "You mean there actually *is* one? It coughs, you say? How odd! There is seemingly no end to life's mysteries. However, I would suggest if the appearance of a dragon confounds you, that you discuss it with the man who is considered the world's living expert on them."

"Who it that, sir?" Jupiter asked.

"Why, my old friend Henry Allen," Mr Hitchcock answered. "I'm surprised he didn't tell you. He used more dragons in his work than anyone before or since."

"Yes, he did mention he'd used dragons," said Jupiter, "but apparently they didn't prepare him for seeing one on his beach. Well, thank you for checking with us, Mr Hitchcock. I think we'd better report our progress to Mr Allen. I'll give him a call."

"No need to," Mr Hitchcock said surprisingly. "I have him on another line at my office. He just telephoned to tell me he was quite impressed with you boys. One moment, and I'll ask my secretary to switch him over."

There was a moment's pause, and then the boys heard the voice of the old film director.

"Hello, is that you, young Jones?" he asked.

"Yes, Mr Allen. I'm sorry to say that so far we haven't found a clue to your missing dog. But we aren't giving up."

"Good lad," Mr Allen said. "Actually I didn't expect results so soon. It's possible that my dog was simply picked up by a stranger and taken away. As I told you, he is an extremely friendly animal."

"We've taken that possibility into consideration, sir," Jupe said. "Have any of your neighbours recovered their missing dogs yet?"

"No," Mr Allen replied. "And I see what you're driving at, young man. The coincidence is still there, isn't it? That all our dogs disappeared at approximately the same time."

"Yes," Jupe said.

"Have you spoken with any of my neighbours?"

"Only the ones you mentioned who don't own dogs," Jupiter replied. "Mr Carter and Mr Shelby."

"Did they have anything to say?"

"They're rather strange neighbours, Mr Allen," Jupe said. "Mr Carter was very angry at being disturbed and threatened us with his shotgun. He doesn't like dogs. It appears they have been tracking over his garden, and he implied he was out to get them."

Mr Allen laughed. "Just bluster, my boy. Carter makes a lot of noise. I don't believe he'd go so far as to shoot a helpless animal. How did it go with my friend Arthur Shelby?"

"Well," Jupe replied, "he was a little better, but not much. He had his own ways of scaring us."

The old film director laughed again. "Oh, you're referring to those devices around his house for scaring off trespassers and pedlars. I suppose I should tell you that Arthur Shelby is quite a prankster."

"Tell him we've already found that out," Bob whispered.

"Perhaps he's trying to remind me that I'm not the only one around who can scare people," Mr Allen continued. "He knows of my old horror films, and maybe he's trying to give me a dose of my own medicine." He chuckled again. "As a matter of fact, Shelby's peculiar sense of humour once cost him an important job with the city. The city fathers didn't appreciate it."

Jupiter glanced at his companions. They all hunched closer in their chairs to hear better.

"What happened?" Jupe asked, trying to keep his voice casual.

"It was several years ago," Mr Allen said. "Shelby is an engineer. He worked with the City Planning Bureau. Knew how the city worked, you might say. One day he decided to take advantage of that fact."

"How?" Jupe asked. "What did he do?"

Mr Allen chuckled again. "It happened on his birthday. It was Shelby's own idea of a jest. Nothing really serious happened. What he did was manage to have all the city traffic lights disconnected at the same time. He said it was his idea of having a birthday cake without candles. Needless to say, city traffic was a hopeless snarl. Businessmen were late for appointments, and late going to work and returning home.

"It was only a temporary blackout—lasted only a few hours. But it raised a lot of indignation that something like that could happen in our busy, modern city. A lot of very important people were quite angry and resolved to get the person responsible. Oddly enough, Shelby admitted it. Said right out he did it to celebrate his birthday—just for the laughs."

"What did they do to him?" Jupe asked.

"Fired him, of course. And they saw to it that he was never again able to secure another job working for the city. He's like me in a way, a man who's been denied his livelihood."

"You mean, he can't make a living any more?" Jupiter asked.

"It hasn't been easy for him," the old man admitted. "Sometimes he does an occasional odd job for some business concern that needs advertising. Electrical signs that move or animate in a clever way. Things of that nature. Not much. He's had to pay for his private joke, you see."

"How about Rose Bowl parades?" Jupiter asked. "Did Mr Shelby ever make any of the floats for them?"

There was a brief silence. Then Mr Allen's voice returned, hesitating slightly. "Not to my knowledge. The floats are displays done in flowers. Shelby's work is more mechanical. Also the Rose Bowl people take their parades seriously. A lot of people pay for seats to watch the floats parade in Pasadena, and they appear on TV. No, young man, I doubt very much that a joker with the past reputation of Arthur Shelby would have been hired for that sort of thing."

"Too bad," Jupe said. "Well, anyway, he makes a lot of things for his own amusement now, and he says they don't hurt anybody."

"Some people don't like his kind of practical jokes, my boy. It's as simple as that. Well, goodbye for now—"

"Just one question, sir," Jupe said. "That dragon you saw the other night—are you sure it was coughing?"

"Quite sure," the old director said. "A coughing sound."

"And you saw it from the top ridge near your house when it went into the cave in the cliff below?"

"Yes, son. I'm sure of that, too. It was late at night, but I haven't lost my faculties yet, despite my lack of sponsors and films to do lately. I still have better than fair vision."

"Thank you, Mr Allen. We'll be in touch with you."

Jupiter hung up. Then he turned to face his partners.

"Any comments?" he asked.

Bob and Pete shrugged.

"So he told us Shelby was a joker," Pete said. "I could have told him that myself. That bird scared me as much as that dragon in the cave."

"Which brings me to my next observation," Jupe said. "And that is, I have found Mr Allen, whom we are supposed to be working for, not altogether reliable in his statements in so far as the truth in concerned."

"Huh?" Pete scowled questioningly at Jupe.

"He's trying to tell us old man Allen is lying," Bob explained.

"Well, why didn't he say so?" Pete asked, aggrieved. He looked at Jupe. "See if you can tell me in words I can understand what the old boy was lying about."

Jupe nodded. "He stated that he was standing on the top ridge when he saw the dragon entering the cave below."

Pete looked puzzled. "So, what's wrong with that?"

Jupiter shook his head. "The cliff there juts out. It's quite impossible for anybody on the ridge to see the cave, or anything entering it. I noticed it last night."

Pete scratched his head, puzzled. "I don't know. Maybe you're right and he's wrong. Can you prove it?"

Jupiter looked solemn. "I intend to. This evening, when we return to the cave. Perhaps then I shall be able to expose not only Mr Allen's fabrication, but also the hoax of the dragon, as well.

"Don't forget," he continued, "we have several suspects in this case. Men who might know about the tunnel, and who also have a grudge against people. Mr Allen and Mr Shelby both lost their jobs and were prevented from working. Mr Carter, if he's the son of the original tunnel builder, would know about the tunnel, too, and have a grudge to settle with a lot of people. How this ties in with a dragon and with the cave we found, I don't know. But maybe we can discover something in the cave tonight."

"You mean," Pete asked, "we're going back to the cave tonight? Back there? With you-know-what waiting for us?"

Jupiter didn't reply and continued writing on the pad in front of him. Then he reached for the phone. "First, I have to find out something," he said. "I should have thought of it before."

14

Start of a Dragon Hunt

"PLEASE put me through to Mr Alfred Hitchcock," Jupiter said. "You may tell him Jupiter Jones is calling."

Pete and Bob looked blankly at each other, then at Jupe. He ignored their questioning glances, as he cradled the telephone with one hand and continued writing notes with the other.

After a moment, he heard the hearty voice of the famous film director. "Alfred Hitchcock here. Am I to take it that you have just solved the enigma of the disappearing dogs at Seaside?"

Jupiter smiled. "Not quite, Mr Hitchcock. I'm calling in reference to what you said a while ago. You mentioned that your old friend Mr Allen was an expert on dragons, and used them in his horror films."

"Indeed he did," replied the director. "Bats, were-wolves, vampires, ghouls, zombies, dragons—anything calculated to scare a human being out of his wits! It's too bad they were all made long before your time. I can assure you that fans still tremble today and get goose-pimples, merely thinking about them."

"So I've heard," Jupiter replied. "I imagine that for Mr Allen to have achieved such effects, these monsters and creatures he used must have looked quite real."

"Of course they did," Mr Hitchcock said crisply. "You don't frighten people with weak imitations of things that are supposed to be frightening, lad. It has to look and act exactly like the real thing."

Jupiter nodded. "Who makes them?"

Mr Hitchcock laughed. "We have very clever studio prop men, naturally. Sometimes a horrendous creature is animated by some ingenious mechanical device inside, motor driven or through gears and a crank. At other times, depending upon the action required of it, we use a different technique. We move the creature a bit at a time and photograph it, and then again and again until we have made it do whatever is required. That is called the 'stop-motion' technique, for your information. When all the frames are run off together, the action seems continuous, you see."

"I understand," Jupe said. "And what happens to the monsters that were created, after the picture is completed?"

"Sometimes they are put away," Mr Hitchcock said, "and saved for another occasion. Sometimes they are sold to an auction house. Other times, they are simply destroyed. Does that answer your question?"

"Yes," Jupe said. "But I have another. Do you have any of Mr Allen's films available that we could see? One particularly to do with dragons."

"Odd you should ask that," the director said, after a moment's pause. "I've been looking through our film library for an old classic of his entitled *Creature of the Cave*, one that is almost entirely to do with a dragon. I've been meaning to make a close study of it for my next picture. Not that I intend using Allen's ideas," he added hastily, "but merely to assure myself that my picture will have to be very good indeed to beat his."

"It would be most helpful to us, Mr Hitchcock," Jupe said quickly, "if we could see this film. I would like very much to see for myself how a real dragon is supposed to look and act. Could you arrange it?"

Mr Hitchcock didn't hesitate a moment. "Be at my studio in an hour. I shall be at Projection Room Four."

The phone went dead. Jupiter put it down on its cradle slowly. He turned to Pete and Bob.

"Remember," he told them. "We will be looking at what is supposed to be an authentic dragon. Pay close attention to the film when we get there. Perhaps you may notice something that might save our lives later."

"What could that be?" Bob asked.

Jupiter got up and stretched. "I've been going on my theory that the dragon at Seaside is a fake. Perhaps I'm wrong. In that case, our dragon is real!"

Promptly on time, transported by Worthington in the grand old Rolls-Royce, The Three Investigators arrived at the bungalow on the Hollywood studio marked as Projection Room Four. Mr Hitchcock, seated at the rear with his secretary, nodded hello.

"Lads, take those seats down front," rumbled Alfred Hitchcock. "I'm just about to signal the projectionist, and we'll get started."

He pressed a button on the seat near him, and the room went dark. Light flickered from a small opening in the booth behind the director, followed by a whirring sound.

"Remember," warned Mr Hitchcock, "this picture was made a very long time ago. The print we are showing is perhaps the only one available. It is underexposed and will be dark and murky in spots. That cannot be helped.

"That is enough introduction. On with the film!"

Soon, the boys forgot where they were. Mr Hitchcock

had not exaggerated. The film was as suspenseful as he had indicated it would be. The story held their attention, and little by little they were led along the path of horror by the skill of the old film director who had made it.

The next scene on the screen dissolved to a cave. The next moment they were in it. And then, as their hearts pounded wildly again, they saw it once more—the dragon!

It filled the screen as it entered the cave, a grotesque creature, huge and frightening. Its short wings lifted, showing long muscles rippling and writhing like live snakes under its wet scaly skin. Then the small, dark head turned on its long, swaying neck to face them.

The long, powerful jaws opened as it roared.

"Wow!" Pete whispered. He shrank back in his seat involuntarily. "That's real, all right!"

Bob stared at the monster moving closer on the screen, and his hands gripped the arms of his seat tightly.

Jupiter sat quietly, concentrating on every move the screen dragon made.

Spellbound they watched the film until the finish. When the dark projection room was flooded suddenly with light, they were still tense and shaking from the film's impact.

As they walked to the rear of the room, their legs were rubbery.

"Whiskers!" Bob exclaimed. "I'm beat. It was just like last night, all over again. I forgot it was a movie!"

Jupiter nodded. "There's the proof of how a master of horror can achieve his effects. Mr Allen had the skill to make us accept and believe anything he wanted. He scared us all out of our wits with a make-believe dragon on a celluloid film. That was his intention and we let him. That's something we must always remember."

"Well?" asked Alfred Hitchcock. "Can you see now why my friend Allen was once regarded as the master of horror films?"

Jupiter nodded. He had a lot of questions to ask the mystery director, but he saw Mr Hitchcock was busy and his secretary waiting to take notes. Instead, he thanked him for providing the film

"You've seen your film dragon now," Alfred Hitchcock said. "I shall await with great anticipation your solution of the mystery of the one in Seaside "

He ushered the boys out and they headed for the gleaming Rolls-Royce where Worthington waited.

They settled back against the leather seats as the tall chauffeur drove slowly towards the gate.

"You told us to watch the dragon closely," Bob said after a moment, "and I did. I couldn't see any difference between this dragon and ours. Could you, Pete?"

Pete shook his head. "The only thing different was this dragon had a better roar than ours."

"I don't think it had a better roar," Bob replied. "It's just that ours seemed to cough a lot."

Jupiter smiled. "Exactly," he said.

"What do you mean, Jupe?" Pete asked.

"Apparently our dragon in Seaside is more susceptible to bad weather. It seems to have developed a cold."

Bob looked intently at Jupe who was sitting back looking quite content. He didn't trust that look. It meant as he had learned from the past, that Jupe was on to something. Something that had eluded both Pete and himself.

"How could a dragon catch a cold?" he asked.

"They're supposed to live in damp caves and water."

Jupiter nodded. "My thoughts exactly. And in a few more hours when we return, we shall be able to expose the mystery of why our cave dragon coughs. If my theory is correct, it might explain why we were allowed to leave the cave, and are still alive."

Pete thought about this and frowned. "That sounds pretty good, Jupe. But what if your theory isn't correct?"

Jupiter blew out his cheeks. "It had better be," he said. "After all, I'm betting our lives on it."

15

Questions and Answers

PETE suddenly exploded. "Maybe it's time you stopped being so mysterious, Jupe, and told us what's going on. We became The Three Investigators to solve riddles and unexplained mysteries. Nobody said anything about becoming Kamikaze suicide pilots. I like my life. Bob probably likes his, too. How about it, Bob?"

Bob nodded, smiling. "I do, I do! And if I lose it, who will you get to do your research and keep your records? Pete's right, Jupe. What gives?"

Jupe shrugged. "I'm not entirely sure, yet. Naturally I wasn't intending to risk our lives needlessly. But there are times when it becomes necessary to take a chance."

Pete shook his head. "Oh no you don't. You'll have to convince me first. I saw a film the other night that my Dad brought home. One with a lot of his special effects. The scientist hero in it took a chance, too, and I'd hate to tell you what happened to him."

Jupe frowned. "I'd forgotten your father was a special-effects man for pictures, Pete. What was it about?"

Pete grinned. "About bugs."

"Bugs?"

"Ants and beetles that take over the world," Pete explained. "One of those science-fiction films. And believe me, it was as scary as that old picture we just saw with the dragon. These insects were fifty to a hundred feet tall—as high as buildings."

"How did they do that?" Jupe asked.

"They used real insects," Pete replied.

"Come on, Pete," Bob said sarcastically. "Real insects as high as buildings?"

Pete nodded. "My Pop explained it to me. It's a different process from the ones Mr Hitchcock explained to us.

"They photograph real insects through a prism—like a monocle—and then blow them up and super-impose them—photograph them again next to pictures of buildings. Naturally they look real and scary because they *are* real! That's how they do a lot of these pictures about monsters that come from outer space."

Jupiter was pinching his lower lip again, his eyes thoughtful. "Do you still have the picture at your house?"

"It'll be there for at least another week," Pete said. "My Pop even suggested that you and Bob might like to see it. You're invited over, any night. Also, it's free!"

Jupiter looked impatient. "I'm afraid we'll need it sooner than that, Pete." He glanced at his watch, then turned to Pete again. "Is your projector battery operated?"

Pete nodded. "Sure. It works both ways."

Jupe pursed his lips. "Is it your own property, not a loan from the studio?"

"It's ours, all right," Pete said. "Or my Pop's, anyway. Say, what's all this about?"

"It's about saving our lives—and possibly solving a mystery at the same time. Do you think your Dad would loan us your projector and the film you saw, just for tonight?"

Pete blinked. "You mean, to take out?"

"To take out," Jupe repeated. "It sounds like the kind of picture I'd like to show somebody."

Pete rubbed at his nose, and then shrugged. "I don't know. I suppose so, Jupe. I'd have to phone him, of course, to get permission."

"That's great," Jupiter said.

"Okay," Pete said. "But before I try to convince my Pop of anything, I want to know where we are going tonight—and why. I'm tired of being in the dark."

Bob nodded in agreement.

They both looked at Jupiter Jones. For a moment, he tried to disregard their stares. Finally, he shrugged and threw his hands open.

"Very well," he said. "I was hoping to keep my clues and deductions a secret. Mostly because I'm not certain yet if they're entirely correct. And even if they are, I'm still at a loss as to where they lead. This investigation started with trying to locate a missing dog. Since then, we have unearthed other mysteries. None of which appear to have anything at all to do with the mystery of the missing dog or dogs of Seaside. Mr Allen hired us to find his dog, Red Rover. But I have felt from the start that the mystery of the other missing dogs would be cleared up when we found his. That was before we met the dragon."

"What *about* the dragon?" Bob inquired. "You've made it pretty clear you think it's a fake one. How come?"

"Yes," Jupe said. "Even though I panicked and ran as you both did, I have several reasons for doubting the authenticity of the dragon in the cave."

"Give us one, for a starter," Pete said. "What makes you think it wasn't real?"

"Several things. The cave wasn't real. The old tunnel wasn't real. The entrance to it wasn't real. Naturally, given those things to consider, one is inclined to doubt that the dragon is any more real."

"I didn't notice any of those things," Bob said.

"Start with the first cave we entered," Jupe said. "We found some boards and moved one aside to enter the smuggler's cave."

"I remember you were looking at them in a funny way," Bob said. "What wasn't real about them?"

"It was supposed to be an old cave, a hideout for smugglers and pirates. The boards were old—at least some were."

"Some?" Pete asked.

Jupe nodded. "The plank that we moved aside, for one. But there was a long, wide piece of plywood. Plywood, I don't have to remind you, is a fairly recent process in manufacturing wood products. There wasn't any available for pirates or even smugglers."

"Plywood?" Pete repeated. Then he frowned, "Well, maybe. But it doesn't sound like too much proof of anything."

Jupiter went on. "Let's take the next cave. The large one we discovered when Bob found the rock that moved. We still don't know who made that possible. If you recall, we advanced into that cave inland, because there was no other way to go. No outside opening, no mouth to it like the first.

"Then we had to stop. We were confronted by what appeared to be a solid wall at the end. We had hoped this cave would lead to the old tunnel Bob had discovered in his research."

Both his partners nodded.

"I remember you started to scrape away at it with your knife," Pete said, smiling. "What did you find out, aside from the fact that solid rock can ruin a good knife blade?"

Jupiter reached into his pocket. He took out his pocket knife and opened it.

"Notice the grey particles on the blade," he said. "Then smell them."

Pete and Bob did as he suggested.

"Paint!" they both exclaimed in unison.

Jupe nodded, folded the knife, and put it away.

"Walls of old caves are not painted," he said. "And as I scraped the covering away, my blade left a streak in the surface. In my opinion, the wall was not rock at all, but plasterboard—sprayed with a grey paint, with sand and small stones thrown roughly on to the surface to make it look like a real cave wall. Plasterboard is, you know, an industrial material commonly used for walls in houses, or partitions in offices. A lot of it is prefabricated, with built-in textures looking like cork or brick.

"I believe whoever put that wall up was trying to hide a fascinating and perhaps valuable discovery," Jupe said.

"Like what?" Bob asked.

"Something more important on the other side," Jupe said. "Something, I suspect, like the original old tunnel of the uncompleted rapid transport system!"

"That's it!" Pete exclaimed. "Somebody discovered the old tunnel and then closed it up so that nobody else could find it! They thought a fake wall would turn away anybody who managed to get in that far."

"Unless," Bob added, "unless that's the way they closed it up in the first place."

"Prefabricated board isn't fifty years old," Jupe said.

"Maybe not," Bob replied. "But we don't know exactly when the tunnel was boarded up, either. Maybe they did it later. To keep kids and animals out."

Jupe's eyes were thoughtful.

"Possibly, Bob, although I doubt it. However, we now have to consider the third mysterious happening. We were at the wall. I was testing it, I turned to show you what was on my knife, and then—"

Pete nodded, and gulped. "Then the cave opened up and it got lighter all of a sudden, and the dragon came in. I see what you mean." He scratched his head. "At least, I think I do. Maybe you'd better tell me."

"All right," Jupe said. "The cave opened up. How did it open? What made that possible? There was no opening outside that we could see. Otherwise, we certainly would have entered that cave rather than the first one, where Bob fell into the mud-hole."

"Okay," Bob admitted. "We couldn't see any opening. But the dragon knew about it, somehow. Because he managed to open it. Maybe he's a lot smarter than we are."

Jupe raised his hand. "Remember, my theory is based on my feeling that everything was false and contrived. Therefore, the dragon was, too. And if it's smarter than we are, then it's only because the dragon is not really a dragon, but something controlled by some human agency."

Pete blinked. He turned to Bob. "What's he saying?"

Bob shook his head. "I think he's saying our dragon is a robot, not a dragon. Is that it, Jupe?"

"I'm not certain yet," Jupiter admitted. "It may be a robot, or some construction similar to the dragon used by Mr Allen in his old horror film. We'll find out in due course.

"What I *am* certain about, however, is the cave entrance. That, too, was not real. Unfortunately, we never tested it or examined it closely from the outside.

I'm sure that if we do, we'll find it's a fake entrance—built of some lightweight material, just as any fake film set or prop is, covered and painted to make it look real. Anybody could build a fake rock. Whoever did it covered the true entrance to the cave. When he wanted to enter, or wanted his dragon to enter, he merely moved the fake opening aside.

"I'm sure you'll both admit," Jupe added, "that if the city of Seaside wanted to cover up a big cave or a tunnel, they wouldn't use any lightweight, painted boards inside and fake rocks outside. They would have sealed it up solidly—with concrete!"

Pete looked out of the window of the smooth-purring Rolls. He frowned, then nodded. "Maybe you're right, so far. If we go back tonight, we'll test those rocks near the first cave entrance. But rocks don't scare me. What I want to know about is the dragon. Why wasn't it real?"

Jupiter Jones sat back, folding his arms.

"We all saw it about the same time. We were about the same distance away. Our hearing and sight are all on a par. Now what did we hear? What did we see?"

Pete and Bob were silent a moment, thinking.

"I heard a humming sound," Bob said. "Then I saw it."

"I saw a bright light—its eyes were shining," Pete said. "About that humming sound, yes—I think I heard it, too. Just before it roared, anyway."

Jupe nodded. "How did it move?"

"How?" Pete asked. " *Very fast!*"

Jupe turned to Bob. "What do you say?"

"I'm thinking!" Bob mopped his forehead. "I agree with Pete. It came in very fast. Just sort of glided in."

Jupe was watching him intently. "Like the dragon

in the film Alfred Hitchcock showed us? Did it move the same way?"

Bob shook his head. "No. Mr Allen's dragon seemed to walk. Ours just kind of glided."

"My impression, too," Jupe said. "It wasn't flying. It didn't move its feet. It glided. Therefore my deduction—it was built merely to look like a dragon. Made to create a startling and frightening effect.

"And the explanation for its gliding is quite simple. Our dragon moved, or was propelled, on wheels! Don't you remember we saw wheel tracks in the sand when we first came down?"

Pete and Bob looked at Jupiter open-mouthed.

"A dragon on wheels?" Pete repeated. "You mean, that's what scared us half to death?"

"I remember something else," Bob said. "We talked about it before. Mr Allen's film dragon roared. Ours seemed to cough a lot."

Exactly!" Jupiter smiled. "That's what I meant about the human agency behind it. Or rather, I should have said, the human agency inside it."

"What are you talking about now?" Pete asked groaning.

Jupiter smiled. "The man inside our dragon had a cold."

The dignified voice of Worthington interrupted. "We're at the Jones Salvage Yard, Master Jones. Shall I wait?"

Jupe nodded. "Yes, Worthington. Pete has to make a telephone call. Then hopefully we'll go to his house and pick up something. And tonight, we're going back to Seaside."

He glanced at his partners. "Am I right, so far?"

Pete grinned. "I just hope you're right later—when we see the coughing dragon again!"

16

Return to Danger

JUPITER'S respect for Pete's father increased when Mr Crenshaw gave the boys permission to use his projector and the new studio film without questioning their reasons.

"He didn't even warn us about taking good care of it," Jupe said. "I guess he trusts our judgment."

"I don't know about that," Pete replied. I'm the one who lives here. If anything happens to that film or Pop's projector, *I'm* the one who gets it!"

The boys were at Pete's home now, in the den used by Mr Crenshaw for his home movies. Pete was rewinding the spool from the take-up reel. Jupiter had asked for a preview of the film so that he could better judge how effective it would be.

"All set!" Pete called. "Lights out, Bob!"

When the room was in darkness, he pressed the switch and the film began. The wall screen blazed with light, and soon the boys discovered that Pete hadn't exaggerated. The photographed insects were terrifying when blown up to outsize proportions.

The sound track suddenly groaned down to silence, and Pete snapped off the image.

"Lights, please, Bob!" he called. "I'm sorry, but I'm showing you the wrong reel. This part comes later. I guess my Pop was running it through again to check on his effects."

He was rummaging through the stack of cylindrical

cans marked with various numbers when Jupe stopped him.

"I don't think it matters, Pete. We don't have to see the entire film now. This part showing the insects in natural surroundings is exactly what I had in mind."

"But that's Reel Six," Pete answered. "It's a flashback. That's just the ants themselves, in the hills and along the shore, getting ready for their invasion of our cities." He picked up another can. "This first reel shows them attacking the cities. The part I mentioned where they're as tall as buildings."

Jupiter shook his head. "We can't show buildings or cities. We want to make it appear as if the giant ants have invaded the cave!"

Pete and Bob looked at Jupe, surprised.

"Is that where we're going to show the picture?"

Jupe nodded. "With the built-in speaker in your projector, we'll have all the sound effects. The wide-angle lens I noticed will be very effective, too. And most important of all, your projector is battery operated so we can run it in the cave."

"We're lucky about that," Pete said. "The battery pack was specially made so my Dad could use it on location work."

Bob broke in. "Well, let's see the rest of this reel you have on now, Pete. Jupe and I can always come back some other night to see the rest of it."

Pete shrugged. "It's okay with me if you fellows like to see a picture backwards."

Bob put out the lights, and Pete resumed showing his film of the giant insects. The boys watched in absorbed silence from then on, giving way to only an occasional murmur of surprise or horror. When it was over, they sat back tingling with excitement.

"Whiskers!" Bob exclaimed. "That's some picture. I can hardly wait to see the whole thing."

Pete pressed the button to rewind the spool, and glanced at Jupiter. "Will that be enough, do you think?"

Jupiter smiled. "It should be perfect for our needs."

"Great," Pete said. "Only I still don't understand what you intend doing with it. Who's going to see it in the cave? That dead man, or ghost, who phoned us?"

"Perhaps," Jupe admitted. "But my main purpose is to find out how a joker responds when a joke is played on him instead."

"A joker?" Bob said. "I didn't think that Mr Carter was joking when he threatened us with his shotgun."

"I wasn't referring to Mr Carter," Jupe said, calmly.

"You weren't?" Bob asked. "Maybe you forgot that he could be the living descendant of the Carter I read about. Labron Carter, who lost his fortune building the tunnel at Seaside and then killed himself because he was ruined. You said yourself, he would certainly know about the old tunnel and cave. And that he might want to get even with the people at Seaside for ruining his father. And, with his kind of temper, he's the kind of guy who could sure do it, too!"

Jupiter shook his head. "Mr Carter's not the man I suspect of creating the dragon in the cave."

"Why not?" Pete interrupted. "What makes you so sure?"

"One thing," Jupe said. "When we met Mr Carter, he did a lot of yelling. But he didn't have a cold. We met a man who was very clever about making things that scared people. If you recall, he did have a cold. And I associate him with the dragon because, as you will remember, *it coughed!*"

Bob blinked. "You think Arthur Shelby is the joker

who made the dragon? I mean—if it's really a constructed one, and not real!"

Jupe nodded. "It could be Mr Allen, too. He knows a lot about dragons. But my guess is Shelby."

"But why Shelby?" Bob asked. "He made scary things to keep people from bothering him at his home. What does he have to do with the cave? It's not his."

"That's what we intend to find out this evening," Jupe said. He glanced at his watch. "I suggest we get ready."

"You're forgetting somebody else," Pete said. "You two are only guessing about Carter, Allen or Shelby. But there were two other men there, and we all saw them!"

"That's right!" Bob said. "The skin divers! And they said something about having to continue their work, before they disappeared."

Pete snapped the big box that locked up the projector. Then he glanced at Jupiter.

"Well?" he demanded. "Am I wrong? What about those two tough guys? Couldn't they have something to do with it?"

Jupiter nodded. "They certainly could. And, if they turn up tonight my suggestion is—project your film for *their* entertainment."

"What about the dragon?" Pete asked. "It might be there, too, you know."

Jupe nodded again. "That should be even more interesting. We've all heard how a mouse can frighten an elephant. It remains to be seen if an ant can scare a dragon!"

It was dark on the ridge above the beach at Seaside. The narrow, secluded street was quiet as Worthington eased the Rolls-Royce close to the kerb and stopped.

Bob stepped out first. He glanced quizzically along the quiet street. "Why so far away this time, Jupe?" he asked. "You've left us a good walk to the staircase."

"Merely being cautious," Jupiter replied. "The Rolls-Royce might have attracted attention here already. If Hans were available this evening, his truck might have provided better cover."

Pete staggered out, swinging the projector in its case. He looked at the long walk ahead of him and groaned. "Don't mind me. By the time I get there with this load, my arms will reach the ground."

"That wouldn't be too bad," Bob said smiling nervously. "You'd pass for an apeman, then. Maybe you'd scare our dragon!"

Pete grunted in reply, and shouldered the case.

"Wait, Pete, we'll give you a hand with that," Jupe offered.

The tall boy shook his head. "No, thanks. I can make it. It's my responsibility. I guess I'll be stuck with it all night, considering I'm the only one who knows how to work it."

Jupe smiled. "Your contribution may prove to be the deciding factor this evening, Pete. Let's hope it works!"

They left Worthington to wait in the car and moved swiftly along the deserted street. Dark clouds obscured the moon. Below they could hear the booming of the heavy surf as it thundered on the beach.

Pete glanced up at the sky nervously. "I wish it wasn't so dark tonight."

"We're all nervous," Jupe admitted. "But darkness is our best protection until we reach the cave."

They were perhaps twenty paces from the staircase leading down to the beach when they heard footsteps.

"Quick! Hit the ground!" Pete urged.

The Three Investigators hurled themselves to the side and rolled behind the thin bushes bordering the sandy vacant ground.

The footsteps came closer along the path. They sounded heavy, confident, and aggressive. Then they slowed and became softer, stealthier. The boys huddled closer, and hugged the ground. Somebody was stalking them!

From the shadows, they were able to see the figure as it came closer. Soon it was almost abreast of them. They stared in fright.

They had seen that bulky figure before. And as they saw it again, their eyes automatically travelled down his body. They recognized the object held close to it.

The menacing shotgun. The one that carried the biggest load of shot possible. The double-ought gun of Mr Carter, the man who hated dogs, kids and seemingly everything.

The disagreeable, hot-tempered man slowed his walk still more when he came level to them. They could see his head swinging suspiciously to the side as he squinted into the darkness. His eyes were black and angry, his lips set in a firm, tight line.

"That's funny," they heard him mutter. "Could have sworn I saw something moving—"

He shook his big head as if puzzled, then continued his walk. The cowering boys waited until they could no longer hear his footsteps before lifting their heads.

When they did, he was gone.

"Whew!" Bob breathed. "Am I glad he didn't see us!"

"Me, too," Pete said. "I guess he even goes to bed with that shotgun in his hand. I wonder who he's looking for?"

"Come on," Jupe whispered. "He's far enough away.

Now's our chance to slip down the staircase. Keep low."

Quickly, they ran the remaining distance to the stairs. "All clear!" Pete signalled.

They hurried down the many steps as silently as they could. When they got closer to the beach, they relaxed. The rolling breakers were making so much noise that they knew their footsteps could not be heard.

Pete reached the sand first. "Okay. Here we go again. I can't wait to find out how that dragon in the cave likes science-fiction movies!"

"We'll find out soon enough," Jupe said, "if he's home."

"It's okay with me if he's not," Bob said. "All I want to find out about is the tunnel. You two can have the dragon."

They came to the original cave they had entered. To the surprise of his partners, Jupe continued walking past.

"Psst! You passed the cave," Bob whispered.

Jupe nodded silently. He pointed ahead to the bluff jutting out to the beach.

"Round the cliff is the entrance to the big cave. We'd better see if it's open or not."

They rounded the bend in the cliff wall and stopped. Three giant-sized boulders crowded against the cliff wall, towering over their heads.

"Those are probably the fake rocks that mask the entrance," Jupe whispered. "Apparently it's closed now."

Pete approached the largest boulder. He put his ear close to it and then tapped it with his hand.

The sound he produced was dull and muffled.

Pete smiled. "You're right, Jupe. It's not solid rock— just like the props made at the studios. Made out of light balsa wood framing, or plaster over wire."

Jupe nodded and turned back. "We'll get you set up in the cave first, so Bob and I can look round."

"What?" Pete spluttered. "Leave me alone while you two—"

"You'll be a lot safer than Bob and me," Jupe said, leading the way back into the smaller cave. "We'll be doing some dangerous investigating. All you have to do is sit tight. And get ready to show your picture."

Pete continued to look puzzled. He looked round. "Who am I going to show it to? Are there any bats flying round here for tonight's audience?"

Jupe had already removed the board leading to the small inner cave pocket. He crawled through and Bob and Pete followed. Then, carefully, they replaced the board.

Jupe whistled softly. "The equipment we forgot last time is still here! Try to find the spot that moves the rock, Bob. We'll pick our stuff up later when we leave."

Bob stooped over the rock in the wall. "Got it," he said happily.

With a slight rumbling sound, the rock turned in the cave wall.

"Here is where you'll stay, Pete," Jupe said. "Inside this small cave. Use the opening in the wall for projecting your film. We're going to wedge the rock in place now so it won't close. When you get the signal, flash your picture on that big grey wall we found inside."

Pete settled down to get his machine ready. He picked up the can of film, then flicked his torch on. "Okay. What will the signal be?"

Jupe thought briefly. "*Help*, I imagine," he said.

17

Mystery of the Old Tunnel

LEAVING PETE BEHIND, Bob and Jupe advanced slowly through the huge vaulted cavern. The air was damp and cold, and they shivered.

They hadn't gone far when Bob whispered, "It's not all there!"

Jupe blinked. "What?"

Bob moved his torch beam ahead, and then swung its light from side to side.

"That big wall—it's—it's open in the centre!"

Jupe followed the arc of Bob's torch with interest. The opening in the grey wall extended from floor to ceiling.

"Bob, I think we've found your lost tunnel!" he cried softly.

Cautiously, the boys stepped through the opening.

The tunnel gradually became larger. It seemed to extend smoothly inwards as far as they could see. Then both boys stopped, their skin prickling, their hearts suddenly pounding.

A huge, shadowy figure was facing them, lying very still and quiet.

It appeared to be waiting for them!

The boys threw themselves flat on the ground, trying not to move, hardly daring to breathe.

They waited and waited. Nothing happened.

The dragon lay there, crouching, a long, dark, humped frightening figure. Its head drooped downwards on the end of its long neck.

"M-maybe it's sleeping," Bob whispered.

Jupe shook his head. He tried to keep his voice low and calm. "Remember," he breathed in Bob's ear. "It's not a real dragon."

Bob nodded curtly. "I know. That's what you've been telling us. Let's hope you're right."

The boys waited another long moment. Then Jupe flicked his light on again, and ran its beam along the ground.

He smiled now, relieved.

"Look at the dragon's feet, and tell me what you see."

Bob stared along the yellow path of light. He blinked.

"Tracks," he said. "Right under the dragon. They look like railway tracks."

Jupe heaved a sigh of relief.

"We were both right. The dragon's a fake, all right. And you've found the underground rapid transport railway that Labron Carter built more than fifty years ago. But you were wrong about one thing, Bob. You said it had never been used!"

"What do you mean?"

"The dragon's been using it," Jupe replied.

"But why? I don't get it," Bob answered, puzzled.

Who would build a dragon to lie in an underground railway tunnel that hadn't been used for fifty years? A railway that wasn't going anywhere. One that would probably never be used again. It didn't make sense.

Why? Bob wondered.

"We're going to find out now." Jupe was tugging at his sleeve. "Let's go before they return."

Bob followed Jupe slowly. "Before who returns?"

Jupe didn't answer. He kept going.

They came up to the monstrous shape huddled in the centre of the tunnel.

Jupiter frowned, puzzled.

"What's wrong?" Bob whispered.

"I can't figure it out," Jupe admitted. "It's facing the other way. Outwards, towards the beach. The fake inside wall is open, yet the outside cave entrance is still closed. What do you make of it?"

Bob shrugged. It wasn't too often that Jupe was stumped and asked what *he* thought about a puzzling situation.

"It looks like whoever's in this thing is heading out—to sea, maybe. But meanwhile they don't want anybody coming in," Bob said.

Jupiter nodded, his eyes bright. "I think you've made an excellent deduction, Bob. Let's look over this remarkable dragon now, before it gets away from us. It could be our last chance."

The drooping head of the dragon lay still as they circled it warily. The eyes appeared closed, lifeless.

Jupe flicked his light against it briefly.

"Hmmm," he said. "They're not eyes at all, but small headlights! Remember how the cave lit up the last time when it entered? And how it created the illusion of blazing eyes?" Jupe chuckled. "It's very simple. All they had to do was use lights, running lights, like a ship, or plane, or train."

They were at the side of the still dragon now. Jupe extended his arm. His fingers seized something that gleamed oddly in the dark, scaly skin.

"Door handle," he muttered. "That's odd. I don't see any door."

Bob peered over Jupe's shoulder. He pointed upwards. "There's another one above it. And another above that."

Jupe laughed shortly. "Fooled me again. It's not a door handle. These are metal ridges to put your feet on. I'm climbing up."

Bob followed Jupe up the footholds. When Jupe was at the top of the dragon, he lifted something up and held it there. He looked down, his lips parted in amazement.

"It's a hatch," he whispered to Bob. "Stand guard. I'm going down to take a look."

Bob gulped and nodded. Jupe heaved his stocky body. Then he was gone. The hatch slowly closed.

Bob started as he heard a thump inside.

It was as if the dragon had finally swallowed Jupe, Bob thought nervously.

He peered into the darkness ahead. In the light of his torch he could see the tunnel curving slightly in the distance. The tracks disappeared as the rounded wall cut off his view. The sides of the tunnel were smooth, showing ribs of steel extending to the ceiling, and patches of concrete.

He heard a rustling noise and jumped.

The hatch had opened.

"Take a look," Jupe urged softly.

Bob clambered up quickly. As Jupe dropped below him, his feet found a narrow ladder. When he touched bottom, Jupe flashed his light round the interior.

"Neat, isn't it? It looks like a dragon. It runs on tracks like a train. But look at this—a periscope! And this porthole. Unless I'm very much mistaken, Bob— this dragon is actually a midget submarine!"

Bob rapped the curved side wall. He rubbed his knuckles. "Whatever it's made of, it's pretty hard stuff."

Jupe nodded. "It would have to be iron or steel in order to remain submerged. But I don't think it is. Let's see what the engine room is like."

The boys walked forward down a narrow aisle.

"Gearshift, dashboard, brakes and pedals!" Bob exclaimed. "What kind of a sub is this?"

Jupe snapped his fingers. "I remember reading of one of the first submarines ever built. It ran along the ocean floor like a car. The inventor had windows built in the sides so people could look out, and charged his passengers admission. There were special air compartments in it to withstand the water pressure.

"The dragon builder might have taken his idea from that or the Rose Bowl floats—mounted on a car chassis, covered by the roses and design of the float. They travel in low gear, directed by a driver hidden below."

Bob snapped his fingers excitedly. "So that's how the dragon moved along the sand without seeming to. I mean, its legs didn't work like the dragon in the film Mr Hitchcock showed us."

"It's understandable," Jupe said. "Mr Allen needed a more realistic type of dragon for the film he directed. The builder of this one just needed something that looks like one. Just enough to get the scare effect he wanted. Only I wish I knew why—or who he's trying to scare."

Suddenly an eerie sound floated through the dragon.

"*Aaaaa . . . ooooo . . . oo!*"

Both boys jumped.

"What was that?" Bob whispered.

Jupiter hesitated. "It came from the rear section."

Bob looked at him. "Are you sure? I don't want to be in this thing if it suddenly decides it wants to take a dip in the sea."

The moaning sound came again, long, drawn-out, and chilling.

"*Aaaaaaahh . . . ooooooo . . . oooo!*"

Bob shivered. "I don't like the sound of that."

To his amazement, Jupe turned and trotted down the narrow aisle to the rear of the dragon. He stopped. The moaning sound came again. Jupe listened carefully, his head bent low to the floor.

"W-what is it?" Bob asked nervously, coming closer.

Jupiter didn't answer. He turned and directed his torch beam along the interior wall of the dragon. Then to Bob's surprise, he smiled.

"I believe we've finally solved our mystery," he said with a chuckle.

"We have?"

Bob cocked his head, listening intently. "I hear it," he said. "I still don't like the sound of it."

"That's because you've allowed your fear of the dragon to overcome your senses," Jupe said, smiling. He opened a narrow door and flashed his light inside the dark opening.

The moans became louder.

Bob blinked suddenly. "Hey—wait a minute! That sounds like—"

He craned his neck and looked inside. His jaw dropped.

"Dogs!" he exclaimed. "Whiskers! A whole cupboard full of dogs!"

"That's the mystery solved," Jupe said. "The mystery of the missing dogs."

"What's wrong with them?" Bob asked. "They look as if they're too sleepy to move, unless they're ill—"

Jupiter shook his head. "Not ill. Sleepy, perhaps. My deduction is they've been tranquillized!"

"Tranquillized?" Bob repeated. "Why?"

Jupe shrugged. "Perhaps they got in somebody's way. And he didn't want to hurt them. Scientists often stun an animal with a tranquillizing dart or needle to render it harmless so they can examine it."

One of the dogs moaned again. "*Aaaaahhh . . . oooooo . . . oo!*"

"That's an Irish setter," Bob said excitedly. "It must be Mr Allen's dog!"

"Red Rover!"

The red-coated dog stretched and yawned. Then it got to its feet and shook its head, its long ears flopping.

"Red Rover!" Jupe called. "Come on out, boy. Come on."

He extended his hand, palm up. The dog looked at it, sniffed and started to wag its long tail.

It took a few tentative steps, staggered and then, regaining its balance, walked out of the cupboard. Then it was rubbing its muzzle against Jupe's knee and whining softly.

"Nice fellow," Jupe said, stroking its head. "Good dog!"

Bob smiled. "Mr Allen was right—it's a friendly dog, all right!"

He extended his hand and knelt. The setter left Jupiter and came to Bob, wagging its tail slowly.

"Good boy," Bob said, rubbing its ears. He looked up at Jupe. "We found it. What do we do now?"

Jupe had taken a slip of paper out of his pocket. He folded it several times. Then he slipped it under the Irish setter's collar.

Jupe leaned forward, until his head was close to the big dog's ear. "Go home, boy!" Jupe ordered. "Home!"

The dog craned its head, and wagged its tail happily.

"Home!" Jupe repeated, extending his arm.

The dog uttered a happy bark. At the sound, other moans and whines came from the open cupboard. Slowly the other dogs emerged, walking stiffly, their tails wagging.

Bob grinned. "Whiskers! I counted—six! We've found them!"

Jupe nodded. As each dog wobbled out, he bent and folded a piece of paper under its collar.

"They're wide awake now. Hand them up to me."

"What's that about?" Bob asked.

"I prepared a brief message for each dog owner in the event we found the dogs," Jupe replied. "Like other successful firms, I think our organization should advertise and get credit for public service."

Red Rover whined.

Jupe turned and knelt. "All right, Red Rover. You're going home first."

He lifted the big dog and carried it up the ladder.

"Home, Red Rover. Home!" he whispered in its ear.

The setter whined happily and scrambled over the top. With long bounds, it raced for the wall opening.

Jupe grinned. "He's wide awake now. Hand the others up to me, Bob. Maybe the fresh air outside will revive them."

One by one, Bob passed them up and Jupe released them. They all came to life soon and ran off after the setter.

Bob brushed off his hands. "Pete can let them out of the cave. Okay, that accomplishes our mission. I'm ready to leave now myself."

His mouth opened in surprise as Jupe lowered the hatch and came down. "We can't leave," Jupe said.

"Why not?" Bob demanded.

"I just saw shadows moving on the tunnel wall. Somebody is coming this way."

"Oh, no!" Bob exclaimed. "We're trapped! Where can we hide?"

Jupe was walking down the narrow aisle. He opened the door of the small cupboard that had contained the dogs.

Pete rubbed his arms to get the chill off. He had already finished setting up the projector. A small rock had been wedged in place to hold the big turning rock firmly open. The reel of film was on the spool, and he crouched nervously waiting for the signal. Then he would flick the starter switch and run the picture.

He fussed once more with his machine to make sure it was aimed at the correct angle through the rock opening. Then he stretched out face down and waited.

He heard a sound behind him, and his flesh crawled. He froze, listening intently. He heard it again.

Somebody, or something, was in the shallow outer cave they had entered first. He was able to hear it now, moving inside. Then, after a long wait, he heard the sound returning.

He heard a scuffing sound in the sand. Then he saw something that made him tremble still more. A big board hiding his smaller cave was moving.

Pete bit his lip. Reluctantly, he reached for his father's projector and pulled it back. He was on his knees now, wondering what to do. There was still time for him to wriggle through the rock opening. He could join Bob and Jupe in the big cave, and let the rock close behind him.

But they were depending upon him to hold his post, he remembered. Those were Jupe's instructions.

The big board moved again. It opened slowly.

Pete moved away until his back was against the cave wall. He waited, watching the boarded opening to the cave give way to the intruder.

Desperately, his hand searched the cave floor, seeking a weapon. Then he remembered his torch and his hand closed on it. The darkness of the cave might not be enough protection.

Then the big board was thrust aside. A burly form stood silhouetted in the faint light of the opening. It was so large that it had to turn sideways to enter the small cave.

Pete sucked in air.

He recognized the ill-tempered Mr Carter and his shotgun.

The roof of the cave was low, and Mr Carter had to stoop to advance farther. He bent and took a step forward. Then he stopped, listening.

Pete heard it, too, his heart pounding wildly.

"*Aaaaaahh . . . ooooo . . . oo!*"

He shrank against the wall. He drew up his legs and gripped his weapon tighter.

Then he heard something else, the sound of running feet. It came closer, accompanied by a panting breath.

Other feet were following. Again he heard the moaning, wailing sound. "*Aaaaahh . . . ooooo . . . oo!*"

It had to be Jupe and Bob running. And being chased.

He gulped. He couldn't close the moving rock now. It was their only way out of the big cave. Their only chance for safety.

But how safe was it? Pete wondered, with the terrible-tempered Mr Carter standing crouched a few feet from him in the darkness, his shotgun at the ready.

There was a sudden whirling, skidding movement. Yellow eyes blazed in the opening in the rock.

Something moaned and bolted through.

It was followed almost immediately by something dark and growling. Then another. And another.

Pete's mouth gaped open as he shrank against the cold cave wall.

He had been prepared for a dragon. This was a pack of wild, furry animals.

Mr Carter grunted as something hit him.

He went down. Pete swallowed nervously. After the pack attacked the fallen man, they would be upon him.

He lifted the torch in his hand.

18

Caught!

BOB AND JUPITER huddled inside the narrow cupboard, straining their ears to hear.

"That's a lot of track to check and clear," a man's voice complained. "As if we didn't have enough to do with all that drilling. But we're all set now."

"It'll be worth the trouble, Harry," another deep voice said. "Let's move it."

"Sure," the first man replied. "He's a slippery character, Jack. Do you think we can trust him?"

The other man laughed. "There's only one of him, brother. And there's two of us. It's our boat. Maybe he ought to be worrying if he can trust us!"

The hatch opened and the men climbed down the ladder. Bob and Jupe, their ears pressed tightly against the thin door, heard one of them walking forward.

An engine whined and caught. They felt a sudden jerk and a slight bump. Then they were moving smoothly on the rails.

Bob touched Jupe's knee in the darkness. "They sound like those two skin divers. Are we going into the ocean?" he whispered.

"I don't think so," Jupe said softly. "There's still not enough ballast in the dragon to keep it submerged."

"Whew!" Bob sighed. "That's a relief."

The dragon moved with only a slight swaying motion to indicate its progress.

"We're going backwards," Jupe whispered, "into the old tunnel."

"I know," Bob whispered. "But why? What are they up to?"

Jupiter shrugged. "I wish I knew. Whatever it is, it sounds important."

The dragon stopped suddenly with a lurch, and Bob and Jupe fell back, bumping against the thin wall.

The man who had been driving came back. "Okay, Harry," his voice rasped. "It's time to load up. Watch yourself!"

"He'd better not try any tricks on us," the other grumbled. "Or I'll crown him with one of those bars."

"Yeah, sure," the first one said. "Well, that's the chance we're taking. For a million bucks, it's worth it!"

Jupe and Bob stared into the darkness of the tiny compartment. One million dollars? They wondered if they had heard correctly.

The men walked away and climbed the ladder. The hatch opened, and fell back into place with a clanging sound.

Jupe tapped Bob's shoulder. "Let's see what they're up to," he whispered.

Stealthily, they opened the cupboard door.

They had taken only a few steps when they halted abruptly. A man was speaking, his voice hoarse and rasping, his words interrupted by spasms of coughing.

"Hurry it up," he said. "I've taken care of the night watchman with some knockout drops. He'll be out for a few hours. We should have the three hundred bars out of there before he wakes up."

Bob nudged Jupe. "You were right. It's Arthur Shelby. I recognize his voice and his cough."

139

"That's the second mystery solved," Jupe whispered. "The mystery of the coughing dragon. Only one remains."

"You mean this one—what they're doing here?" Bob asked.

"The mystery of the three hundred bars," Jupe replied.

"Three hundred bars of what?"

He tapped Bob's shoulder and moved along the dimly-lit aisle of the dragon again. Then, carefully mounting the narrow steps, he raised the hatch with his hands and peeped out.

His mouth gaped open. He was looking at a concrete wall alongside the dragon. A large hole had been drilled in it—a hole big enough for men to walk through. A man emerged from it carrying something in his arms and leaning back to balance the weight.

"Hey! This stuff weighs a ton," he complained.

"Sure," Shelby answered. "Why do you think you Morgans were hired—just because you have a handy boat? What this job needed was a lot of muscle power. The kind you used drilling our way into the vault. You and your brother were hired to take care of that and the loading from here to your boat."

"Sure," the man grunted. "I ain't complaining. How much does each one of these things weigh?"

"About seventy pounds," Shelby replied. "Just stack them alongside the dragon. When we've got the three hundred out of there, we'll load up the dragon and head for sea."

The husky Morgan brother put his load down and turned back to the hole in the wall. His brother came out, leaning back and breathing heavily.

"Okay, Jack," he grunted. "Three less to go now."

He set his bars down as Shelby directed and returned to the wall and disappeared inside.

Jupiter lowered the hatch.

"Mr Shelby said each bar weighed about seventy pounds," he whispered. "The Morgan brothers were talking about a million dollars. I think I know what those bars are. Gold!"

"Gold?" Bob exclaimed. "Where's it coming from?"

"The large standard gold brick or bullion bar the government makes," Jupe said, "is seventy pounds! The smaller standard gold bar weighs twenty pounds and is worth nine thousand, six hundred dollars alone! Shelby and the Morgan brothers appear to be robbing a Federal Reserve Bank!"

"Whiskers!" Bob exclaimed softly. "How much is one of those seventy pound bars worth?"

Jupe frowned, and calculated swiftly. "Approximately four hundred and eighty dollars a pound . . . times seventy . . . or—" Jupe whistled softly "—over thirty thousand dollars! Thirty-three thousand, six hundred dollars, to be exact!"

"Wow!" Bob exclaimed again. "And Shelby said they were taking three hundred bars!"

"I make that amount to be ten million, eighty thousand dollars," Jupe calculated. "Quite a haul."

"That makes us witnesses to a pretty important bank robbery," Bob whispered. "We'd better get out of here, if we want to stay alive!"

Jupe agreed, his voice husky with excitement. "The question is *how*—Mr Shelby is too close to the dragon!"

He walked forward slowly, thinking. Then suddenly he darted to the head of the dragon.

Bob was right behind him, wondering if Jupe had found a new place for them to hide.

Jupe stopped so abruptly, Bob bumped into him.

"Sorry," Bob murmured, "I didn't expect—"

His companion raised a warning finger to his lips.

He leaned forward, his eyes gleaming with excitement.

"Hold tight!" Jupe whispered fiercely. "They've left the ignition key in!"

Bob's jaw gaped. "You mean—you're going to drive it—away? Can you drive it? How will you see? There's no windscreen".

Jupe shrugged. "It's worth a try. I'm sure this runs like an ordinary car, and I know how a car works. There's a foot clutch, brake, gearshift, accelerator. And it'll be on the tracks to the end of the tunnel."

He dropped to the small seat. "Here goes," Jupe called, and turned the ignition key.

The engine whined shrilly.

It whined again. Then it coughed and stopped.

"It coughed, Jupe!" Bob exclaimed. "Then it wasn't Shelby coughing."

Jupe nodded, biting his lip. "It stalled," he said bitterly. He turned the key again, holding it hard in the lock.

The engine whined once more. Suddenly it caught with a loud roar.

Jupe sighed, relieved. He pulled the gearshift into first and slowly eased his foot off the pedal.

The dragon bucked forward in one convulsive leap. Then it coughed and stopped. The engine was quiet.

"Stalled again!" Jupe cried bitterly. "It's the clutch that—"

Then he and Bob whirled. Something heavy was banging on the side of the dragon. They heard something fall against it with a loud thud. Then they heard something more ominous.

The hatch was opening.

"We should have locked it!" Bob whispered.

Jupe nodded, his eyes frightened. "I know. I'm sorry —I wasn't thinking."

19

A Desperate Situation

PETE TREMBLED. He braced himself against the cave wall, the heavy torch held tightly in his hand. He might get one of the furry animals, he knew, but there were too many of them to fight.

Mr Carter was too big and strong for him, too, even without his deadly shotgun.

Luckily he was down now, fallen under the swift charge of the animals. Pete watched horrified as they went at him. Then he blinked.

There was no attack. The animals leaped over the prostrate Carter and bolted through the gap provided by the opening of the big planks.

Pete sat up, puzzled. He whirled at another eerie moan. Another small beast had entered the cave, its eyes blazing. Before Pete could move, it had leaped over his outstretched legs. It swerved round the fallen man, and ran after the others through the plank opening.

Pete didn't hesitate. Carter didn't appear hurt, only unconscious. He would be wakening soon, with his surly temper and his even more frightening shotgun.

Jupe had given Pete orders to stay, with his projector ready. But he had not ordered him to stay alone and get shot. Maybe there was another way he could help.

He dived for the opening, pushed his projector ahead, and crawled forward. He pulled himself through, then paused to listen. He heard Mr Carter groan.

There was no time now to fiddle with the rock Jupe and Bob had wedged into place. Pete leaped to his feet, grabbed his machine and awkwardly ran forward.

Ahead of him, in the light of his torch, he suddenly saw an opening in the huge grey wall. Instinctively, he darted through.

As he did he heard a strange rustling sound. It was coming from behind him. He whirled, and a chill ran down his spine.

The wall was closing behind him!

His half-hearted leap to retreat failed. The open sides of the walls clicked together.

Another strange sound made him jump. He looked round and his eyes widened. Ahead of him stretched a long, wide tunnel. And far down it, coming straight for him, was a large grotesque shape he recognized. Its yellow eyes blazed wildly. Its mouth opened.

The dragon roared!

Snapping off his light, Pete took a frightened step back. He felt the wall. It was impossible to retreat farther.

He moved slowly into the darkest corner, holding his projector in front like a shield.

He trembled again as he watched the dragon advancing in little hops, fascinated by the swaying head and open mouth. There was no sign of Jupe and Bob. Pete bit his lip and groaned.

Bob and Jupe were undoubtedly in the monster's huge belly. He'd lost his chance to rescue them! And as the dragon came closer, he wondered what his own fate would be.

Arthur Shelby's voice floated down through the open hatch into the dragon. It didn't sound like the voice of a playful practical joker. It was more like a deep-throated growl, full of menace.

"Come out of there, whoever you are, if you know what's good for you!"

Bob looked at Jupe. Jupe shook his head, his lips set in a firm stubborn line.

His hands stabbed wildly at the control buttons.

"This is our only chance, if I can get this darn dragon running!"

The engine caught again. The dragon lurched and jumped forward. The huge neck suddenly swung up in front of them.

Bob gestured excitedly at the sight. "Jupe, look! One of those buttons you hit must have made the head come up. There's an opening to see through!"

Jupe nodded and stepped harder on the accelerator pedal. The dragon suddenly stopped short, coughing, and they heard Mr Shelby cry out.

A clattering sound came from above them, then a dull thud.

"I think we just lost Mr Shelby, Jupe. Keep going!" Bob urged.

"I'll try—but I'm doing something wrong. It keeps stalling!"

He turned the key again and pressed the starter button. Above the whine of the engine, he heard Mr Shelby bellowing for the Morgan brothers.

Bob darted to the rear and pressed his face to the small porthole in the side.

"Here they come, Jupe! They look mad, too. Do something!"

Again the starter caught and the engine hummed. Jupe pressed the clutch in again, pulled the gearshift lever and stepped on the accelerator pedal.

The dragon took a tremendous forward leap.

Then it stalled once more.

Grimly, Jupiter got it started again. The dragon leaped forward. And once again, it stopped with a sickening lurch.

"Keep going!" Bob urged. "Every time you move, you lose them!"

Jupe had started the engine again.

"How far back are Mr Shelby and those two strongmen?" he asked.

Bob turned his head. "Whiskers!" he exclaimed. "Right on top of us! Get going!"

The dragon leaped forward again, glided several feet, and then abruptly coughed and stalled.

Bob looked back. The Morgan brothers were running hard now, their faces contorted with anger. Arthur Shelby was running just behind them, waving his arms wildly.

"Stop them, you fools! Without the dragon, we don't have a chance!"

Spurred on, the husky Morgan brothers increased their pace. Bob paled. Their fingers were almost touching the dragon's long tail. He remembered how easily they had carried the heavy gold bars. If they caught the tail, it could be child's play for them to pull the dragon back!

Jupe heard Bob's warning cry, and got the dragon moving again. But after another series of long convulsive leaps forward, it coughed and stalled.

He pushed the starter button. The engine whirred. It didn't catch.

"It's no use," Jupe said, biting his lip and scowling. "Now I can't even get it started."

"It doesn't matter any more," Bob said dully. "They've caught up with us."

As he had feared, the Morgans had finally managed

to grab the long tail of the dragon. Now he saw them braced, leaning back, holding it still.

Then one of them ran forward.

"Get 'em out of there, Harry!" the other Morgan yelled.

Harry nodded. He leaped for the metal ridges leading to the top of the dragon and the open hatch.

"They got us, Jupe," Bob cried. "What'll we do?"

Jupe sighed. There was nothing else to do. He got up and walked down the narrow aisle.

"Perhaps if we surrender now, they won't hurt us," he said, doubting his words as he said them.

Preceding Bob on the narrow ladder, he held his arms up high.

"We give up, Mr Shelby," he called. "We're coming out now."

He heard Shelby's angry shout. Then another noise filled the cave. It was a roar that echoed and bounced off the thick walls of the tunnel.

"*RR—AAAAAAGHHHHHH!*"

Jupe jerked his head round at the roar and saw the wall ahead of them had closed.

He heard the Morgan brother coming up the side call out, "Watch out, Jack!"

Then, incredulously, he saw the tough faces of the husky men dissolve into astonishment, then into fear. Another frightening roar filled the cave.

Bob grabbed Jupe's arm. "Look!"

Jupe nodded. A huge ant had suddenly appeared on the cave wall. It seemed very far away. Then, with an astonishing leap, it had closed the gap between them, and was almost on them.

Harry Morgan screamed from the top of the dragon. "Monsters! Look out!"

In almost the same breath, he had reached into

his pocket. A gun gleamed in his shaking hand.
He fired twice.

The ant on the wall seemed to scream its defiance, and came closer. Another ant followed, sliding up the tunnel wall to gigantic size, almost filling it.

"I hit him and it went right through him!" yelled the first Morgan. He fired again and again.

The ants roared and kept coming. They came in increasing numbers, filling the cave, crowding the walls.

Arthur Shelby had come up and was staring at the walls, a curious expression on his pale, freckled face.

Both Morgans were firing now.

"Giant ants coming out of the walls," the bigger Morgan yelled. "The bullets don't bother them. Get us out of here, Shelby!"

Shelby shrugged and stared at the moving ants on the wall.

The second Morgan grabbed him, brandishing his pistol. "Open the wall, Shelby, or I'll let you have it. We're getting out of here!"

Shelby looked at him coldly. Then, with a shrug, he reached into his pocket. A thin, tubular object appeared in his hands. He put it into his mouth.

Bob and Jupe waited for the shrill sound of a whistle. They heard nothing. They saw the wall slowly open.

"Come on, Jack!"

The Morgans ran for the opening, firing wildly at the ants on the wall screaming back at them. In another instant they had gone through the huge walls.

"Run, you fools!" Arthur Shelby said mockingly. He looked up at Bob and Jupiter, a curious appraising look on his face.

"Very clever," he said drily. "But a little too clever,

my young friends. You've cost me a fortune, and I don't see how I can decently let you get away with that."

He reached into his other coat pocket. This time he held a more frightening object. His eyes glittered.

"Don't shoot," Bob gasped.

Shelby coldly nodded to them. "Step down, please." And as Jupe came down, followed by Bob, Shelby added, "The next time you try to appropriate a bus-like vehicle, I strongly suggest you learn how to double-declutch when you change gear. Stops stalling you see."

Both boys climbed down. Shelby turned towards the darkest corner of the wall and the cone of light. "And you with that projector," he called. "Shut off that film and come over here, at once! I've a gun in my hand, I warn you!"

The screaming in the cave stopped. The ants flickered on the wall and then disappeared.

"D-don't shoot!" Pete yelled. "I'm coming."

He came up slowly, looking wonderingly at Jupe and Bob standing beside the still dragon

"It's really not real?" he asked Jupe.

Jupe shook his head.

"No more real than your giant ants," Shelby snapped. He looked at the boys and then at the gun in his hand. "I regret this, boys, really I do. But you had no business interfering—"

He halted suddenly, his arm extended and trembling. A loud eerie moan floated through the tunnel.

"*Aaaaaahhhh . . . ooooooohh . . . oooo!*"

"Oh, no! Not again!" Shelby cried. Quickly, he reached into his pocket and produced the slender object he had used before. He put it to his lips. Again it made no sound.

149

The huge walls rustled and closed.

Jupiter, listening intently, smiled. He flicked on his torch.

Caught in his glaring beam, they saw huge, leaping shapes coming at them, their eyes glowing, their jaws open, sharp teeth menacing.

"Look out!" Pete yelled. "Those furry animals—"

Then he gasped and grinned sheepishly. "I mean, dogs," he added. "Wow! What a dope!"

Arthur Shelby groaned too. "Too late," he sighed.

The first animal bounded up to them, barking happily. Its long, brushlike tail swept back and forth in a feverish arc. Its dull reddish coat gleamed.

"Red Rover!" Jupe exclaimed. "He's come back."

The big setter ignored Jupe's outstretched arm and leaped for Shelby. The red-headed man backed off, holding his gun outstretched.

"Go away, Rover," he snapped. "I'm warning you —for the last time—go home!"

The big dog shook its head and whirled round the man. The other dogs came at him, too, backing him up to the wall.

They leaped happily at the man, growling and barking, their tails wagging. Once more, Shelby waved at them with his gun. His face was pale, shining with sweat.

"It's no use, Mr Shelby," Jupe said. "You can't shoot them. You like dogs too much. And they're certainly crazy about you."

The thin, red-headed man regarded the leaping animals and lowered his gun.

"Yeah," he said morosely. "Crazy about me. That's it, all right."

He looked blankly at the slender metal object in his hand, then shrugged and put it back in his pocket.

He put his hand down and almost unconsciously stroked the heads of the happy dogs.

"Now what?" he asked, speaking to himself.

"I've an idea, sir, if you care to listen," Jupe said.

"You have?" The pale eyes stared at the stocky boy.

Jupiter Jones nodded. "Yes, sir. It's based largely on the idea that you're really a practical joker, not a greedy criminal. Would you care to hear it?"

The red-haired man nodded curtly.

"Put everything back. We'll help you, if you like," Jupe said. "You might want to leave the hole you drilled in the wall, just as it is. It will be your joke on them. That you had the chance to take all that gold, and you didn't. We won't tell, and they'll never know who did it—or rather who *nearly* did it!"

20

Alfred Hitchcock Offers a Hand

WHEN Pete, Bob and Jupiter entered Alfred Hitchcock's office two days later, the famous director was seated at his desk, reading a newspaper. He motioned them to his big, comfortable chairs.

"Sit down, boys," he said. "I'll be with you as soon as I finish this interesting article in the papers."

They sat and waited patiently. Finally, the director folded the paper and put it aside on his desk.

"So!" he boomed in his hearty voice. "I suggest a case for you concerning the missing dog of an old friend. And what happens? Not only his, but several others are returned. I also see a column in the Seaside newspaper telling of some bizarre plot to rob a large bank. The heading reads: 'BANK OFFICIALS PUZZLED BY CONTRITE AND CONTRARY CROOKS!' Was this all your doing? I must admit I am puzzled, too."

Jupe cleared his throat. "Yes, sir. It was. They were—I mean, sir—yes, we're kind of responsible for everything."

Mr Hitchcock held up his hand. "Your modesty, lad, is most laudable. Still, I would rather hold my own praise in abeyance until I completely understand how you three solved this unique mystery of the missing dogs."

"Well, sir," Jupe said. "Actually you helped us a great deal in solving the mystery, sir, when you showed us that old film Mr Allen made with the dragon."

152

"Ah, yes," Mr Hitchcock said. "And, as I recall, there was some talk about you boys actually encountering one of those rather fantastic beasts."

"We sure did," Pete said abruptly. "And we're lucky to be alive to tell about it. Even if it *wasn't* real."

"Incredible!" Mr Hitchcock murmured. "The very real menace of a dragon that wasn't real. I should like very much to hear about it."

Bob Andrews whipped out his note book. He proceeded to tell how the investigation had run into a snag at the very beginning, and then how they had managed to pick up the threads that ultimately led to the solution of their original mystery. Mr Hitchcock listened attentively.

"Your Mr Shelby sounds like a most ingenious and interesting man," he said. "Do I understand you correctly when you say he voluntarily gave up his foolproof plan to steal several million dollars' worth of gold, rather than hurt you and some dogs?"

"Yes, sir," Jupiter said. "He kept the dogs alive and fed them. He had to tranquillize them to keep them quiet and out of his way. He told us he was going to turn them all loose when he left the cave for the last time with the dragon and the gold.

"He could have forced us at gunpoint to help him carry out the gold after the Morgan brothers ran away. He could have taken enough to be wealthy. He didn't need the entire ten million dollars."

Mr Hitchcock drummed his fingers on the desk. "And his original plan was actually to run the dragon underwater at night, in conjunction with those villainous Morgans?"

Jupe nodded. "I thought the dragon was too light, but he had calculated his ballast in advance—the heavy gold bars. He had to test his dragon in the water, at first, by loading it with rocks. As a matter of fact, that's how your friend Mr Allen happened to see the dragon. It was out on a test run, while he was looking for Red Rover."

"And your clue to Shelby's part in it was his cold?"

Jupe smiled weakly. "He had a bad cough when we met him. So I associated him with the coughing of the dragon. Later I found out it coughed when it stalled. That was partly due to wet wiring, from the many experiments in the sea."

"But your mysterious phone call—the ghostly, rasping voice—that was really Shelby?"

Jupe nodded.

Mr Hitchcock shook his head. "This Arthur Shelby doesn't sound like a typical crook at all. How did he happen to tie up with such low characters as the Morgan boys?"

"They had a salvage rig and he knew them as tough men who would do anything. He needed their help for the work in the cave, drilling into the bank vault through the concrete wall of the tunnel, and then getting the gold out. When he offered them a million dollars, they were more than willing."

"And how did they propose to get the gold from the sub into the boat?"

"After he got under way, the Morgans with their underwater gear were to attach a cable from the sub to their tug, and tow it out to sea. When they were far enough out, they were going to surface the sub and unload the gold bars. Then they were going to head for Mexico."

Mr Hitchcock nodded. "Why a dragon, at all?"

"That was from knowing your friend Mr Allen and his film background, using dragons to scare people. You see, at first Shelby just thought it would be a new way to play a practical joke on his neighbour. But when he heard of a large shipment of gold bars to that bank, he decided to carry out a robbery. He figured the dragon could easily be converted into a functioning sub. It suited his kind of offbeat thinking—a funny and perfect way to get the gold from the bank through the old tunnel to the sea. It backfired on him because it was the oddity of the dragon that kept us interested in trying to solve the mystery."

"I should have imagined Mr Shelby to be without sufficient funds to construct something as elaborate as that dragon," Mr Hitchcock said.

Bob was ruffling through his notes. "I left out a page," he explained. "He told us he had friends working at some of the studios. Some of them liked to make gadgets like he did. They told him of a prop dragon that was to be destroyed to make room for other properties needed in storage. He saved them the trouble, went down and took it apart there himself. Then he had it hauled to his place in pieces and put it together later."

Mr Hitchcock frowned. "Did it have wheels?"

"No," Bob said. "That was another bargain he picked up. He found an old abandoned chassis from a float at the Pasadena fairgrounds, left over from the Rose Bowl parade. They let him have it for towing it away. He put the dragon on that."

"Hmmm. Clever," Mr Hitchcock said. "Now, how was it that Shelby knew about the big cave and the tunnel, whereas my friend Allen, who lived almost directly over them, did not?"

"Well, to begin with, Shelby knew about the existence of the tunnel from his days as an engineer for the City Planning Board. But he only found a way into the tunnel by accident.

"A landslide from an earthquake had covered the big cave many years before either he or Mr Allen lived there," Jupe continued. "Shelby was walking along the beach one day and saw a fissure in the rock wall. He dug in and discovered the cave and then the tunnel. He told the Morgans. They helped him build the fake wall inside. It was to fool people who accidentally found their way into the cave, and stop them from going farther into the tunnel."

"I assume they helped him make the fake rocks outside the entrance, too?" Mr Hitchcock said.

"Yes," Jupe said. "That was interesting, and well thought out, too. They had to work from the inside of the cave and not attract attention. It was only when they had it all constructed that they could afford to clear the outside rubble away, at night, and insert their own rock covering."

Mr Hitchcock nodded. "The Morgan brothers—were they responsible for the collapsing staircase on your first adventure there?"

Pete interrupted. "They didn't want anybody around who might spoil their scheme, so they weakened that staircase to scare people off the beach. They spotted us from their boat when we fell down it. And when we didn't leave, they came out of the ocean and pointed their spear guns at us. They figured that should frighten us into not coming back."

"I see," Mr Hitchcock said. "I believe you mentioned they had disappeared in the original cave you entered. Did you solve that mystery?"

Bob was back to his missing page of notes. "They went down the same pit I fell in. It wasn't quicksand. Just a lot of mud and water. With their gear, they were able to work their way through to an underground passage that came out in the other cave near the

156

tunnel. Like cave diving. It was an alternative way into the large cave during the day. They couldn't take a chance of disturbing the big rocks outside too much and possibly attracting attention. Incidentally, after they ran out of the cave that last night, they never came back. I guess they were ashamed of being scared."

"And good riddance, I might add," Mr Hitchcock said. "The thin, reed-like object Shelby blew into, that made no sound but opened and closed the fake cave wall. Am I to assume that was a sonic contrivance?"

Jupe nodded. "It opened and closed the prop rock opening outside, too. It had two varying high-frequency sounds. But it was Mr Shelby's undoing actually."

"Indeed, young Jupiter!" Mr Hitchcock exclaimed. "How was that?"

"It was his experimenting with the silent whistle, his sonic beam, that attracted all the dogs to him in the first place. As you know, sir, dogs can hear a higher frequency wavelength than humans. Mr Allen's setter ran to him the first night it was released from the kennel. He didn't expect that because he thought Mr Allen was still in Europe. That meant he had to move fast. The other neighbourhood dogs had already deserted their owners at night and run to Mr Shelby's sonic whistle. He couldn't get rid of them, and had a lot of work to do, getting the dragon ready, the bank-vault opening drilled and the tunnel tracks cleared to the bank. Rather then destroy the dogs, as the Morgans wanted, he merely put them to sleep by adding tranquillizing agents to their food."

Mr Hitchcock reflected some more. "The dragon roared, you said. Was that your imagination running wild, lads?"

Bob shook his head. "No, sir. That roar and a lot of other things, like a windscreen opening in front were controlled by instruments on the dragon dashboard. Jupe was pressing all the buttons he could find in order to get it going."

"Now, this Mr Carter," Alfred Hitchcock asked, "did he get safely out of the cave after being bowled over by the escaping dogs?"

"Yes," Pete interrupted. "He was gone when we went back there to pick up the equipment we'd left behind."

Mr Hitchcock nodded. "And was he actually the living descendant of the Carter who started the tunnel and lost his fortune at Seaside?"

Jupe smiled. "Yes. But although he knew there was a tunnel, he never did find out exactly where. That's why he knew about the first cave, and the boards leading into the next one. He was constantly snooping round there, and was more of a problem and worry to Shelby and the Morgans than we were. I suppose that's why he always carried his shotgun with him, because he suspected something was going on.

"After the staircase near his house collapsed, he got suspicious again and went down to investigate. That's when he nearly ran into Pete.

"Mr Shelby told us the boards in the first cave had evidently been put in a long time ago by smugglers or pirates. He assumed they had built the moving rock. He found it by accident, just as we did. He added the newer plywood pieces himself when some of the old boards rotted. He was afraid somebody else would discover the moving rock and then the big cave and tunnel. He must have been saving the moving rock for a private emergency exit, because he never told the Morgan brothers about it."

158

"And you helped Arthur Shelby return the gold bars to the bank vault?" Mr Hitchcock asked.

"No," Bob broke in. "He thanked us for the offer but said it was his own responsibility. He didn't want to get us involved in any kind of criminal activity.

"He managed to get the gold bars back inside, and left them lying around carelessly as another kind of joke. Then he patched up the hole they'd made. I suppose the bank will eventually discover the tunnel underneath their vaults. But we haven't told anybody else, not even Mr Allen."

Mr Hitchcock nodded. "It is all certainly possible, given a man of Shelby's considerable engineering talents. And it all came about because he knew the complete underground history of the city of Seaside."

"Yes, sir," Jupe said. "And the present-day history, too. So he knew exactly what banks were accessible from the tunnel all the time."

"I see. One thing disturbs me. You allege my old friend Allen lied deliberately, saying he saw the dragon enter the cave, when it was impossible."

"I'm sorry about that, sir," Jupe said. "We found out later it was a simple mistake. He had been halfway down the steps that time, but had forgotten it in his distress at losing Red Rover. Is there anything else, sir?"

"No, boys. Though perhaps I should meet this Mr Arthur Shelby. A man ingenious enough to scare you three lads is a man I could use. After all, you must remember, horror is my business, too."

"Thank you, sir!" Jupiter cried, and Bob and Pete echoed the words. The First Investigator leaped to his feet. "We'd better get going. We've taken up enough of Mr Hitchcock's time."

There was a flurry of happy boys, and then they had gone.

"Mmmm," Mr Hitchcock murmured to himself. "I wonder if I should borrow that ingenious dragon Mr Shelby devised. Since I've just purchased that large bus-like trailer for my holidays, perhaps it would be a good idea if I learned how to double-declutch the dragon in the cave first, before I ventured forth on the Los Angeles motorways!"